I0716393

THIS ENCHANTED ISLAND

TEACUP MAGIC
BOOK SIX

TANSY RAYNER ROBERTS

Copyright © 2024 by Tansy Rayner Roberts

Cover design © 2024 by Merry Book Round

Proofing by Earl Grey Editing & Isabel Dallas

All rights reserved.

No part of this book may be reproduced in any form or by any electronic or mechanical means, including information storage and retrieval systems, without written permission from the author, except for the use of brief quotations in a book review.

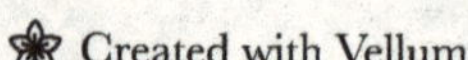 Created with Vellum

For all the mermaids
And the sea witches
Don't lose your heads

CONTENTS

TEACUP MAGIC READING ORDER

MNEMOSYNE SEABOURNE

Tea & Sympathetic Magic
The Frost Fair Affair
Spellcracker's Honeymoon

LADIES OF THE TEACUP ISLES

Lady Liesl's Seaside Surprise
Have Spirit, Will Duchess
This Enchanted Island

DRAMATIS PERSONAE

OF THE *CALIBAN*

Miss Metis Seabourne/Bonny Blythe, *who ran away to sea*

Calypso, *first mate and part-time mermaid*

Captain J. Willoughby Bones, *a man who looks most appealing in black leather*

Sal, *boatswain/bosun, a practical sort*

Ginger, *quartermistress, glamorous and kind*

Jacob Fry, *gunner*

Dr Sebastian "Doc" Smedley, *ship's surgeon*

Rafferty, *ship's cook*

HOBSBAWN, *able seaman & husband*

LILLIT, *able seaman & wife*

DAMON, *able seaman & husband*

TIGRIS, *cabin sprat*

ELPHINY, *cabin sprat*

QUEEN AUD, *monarch of the Teacup Isles, basically a stowaway*

OF THE *ROSALIND*

CAPTAIN ELIZAH BELL, *an old lag with a fast ship*

DONCASTER, *ship's surgeon*

MRS MNEMOSYNE "MNEME" SEABOURNE, *cousin and Queen's lady*

MR C. THORNBURY SEABOURNE, *spellcracker and Queen's man*

BASIL SEABOURNE, *magical glass hedgehog, one of the family*

MR DOMINIC "THE GHOST" VON TRASK, *a necromancer with pale eyes*

ALFRED, LORD MANTICORE, *the Queen's Minister, no one's favourite (except hers), recently divorced*

LADY HADDERINE BUSTLEDOWN, *Mistress of the Robes*

OF THE ISLE OF DREAM

Queen Ianthe, *a sea witch*

Prince Orion, *a bridegroom*

The Riddle, *a mystery wrapped in an enigma*

Thetis, Doris and various other sirens, sea witches, nereids and mermaids, now departed

Various frog butlers, with a secret past

ELSEWHERE

Miss India Tiffing, *a young lady with limited spirit of adventure*

Mr Octavian Swift, *Queen's Consultant*

Henry Jupiter, Duke of Storm, *a cousin who married well*

Juno, Duchess of Storm, *enjoying a well-deserved rest with her feet up & her husband hovering*

Mrs Hecate Seabourne, *Metis' mamma, convict*

Mr Gaulliver Seabourne, *Metis' father, magister*

Mrs Galatea Seabourne, *Mneme's mamma, Metis' aunt*

Decius Hartigan, *former captain of the* Miranda*, retired*

PART I

THE CALIBAN

THE MERMAID

ONE YEAR AND THREE MONTHS AGO

*M*iss Metis Seabourne had held high hopes about running away to sea. She imagined adventures, romance, a little light swashbuckling. As a child, she nursed to her heart the idea of running away to become a pirate, which would of course solve all of her problems.

Her favourite bedtime story had been *The Adventures of Bonny Blythe, Pirate Captain*: a collection of tales about a girl with red hair like her own, who put on trousers and ran away to sea with her pet monkey.

Then, just short of her twenty-first birthday, Miss Metis Seabourne's whole world fell apart. A family scandal ripped through her life, leaving her mamma in the Tower of Thyme awaiting trial, and herself…

For the first time in her life, Metis was free to make choices of her own. She made her plans quickly, before other family members decided she should be their respon-sibility. Her solution was to run away to sea, leaving word only with her cousin Mneme. It was not unheard of for unmarried ladies to tour the Continent after a failed Season, and hers had failed more spectacularly than most.

Metis talked herself into a travelling party with an old school friend, Miss India Tiffing, and set sail on the *Hortensia*, a highly respectable Continental cruise ship.

What she had not taken into account was that if one belonged to that horrendous category of society known as ladies-and-gentlemen, even something as exciting as running away to sea was an awful bore.

Miss Tiffing and Miss Seabourne accidentally fell in with The Right People on board the *Hortensia*. This meant formal dinners at the captain's table every night, the occasional visit to carefully curated seashore attractions along the endless coast of the Continent, and interminable supper entertainments, deck games, and themed dances.

Having joyfully escaped a world of house parties, garden parties and the Season, Metis quickly discovered that travelling as a gentlewoman included the worst aspects of all those things with the added disadvantage that one was *trapped on a boat*. At least she had India, a dear companion who kept Metis sane through the tedium thanks to her wry observations and self-deprecating sense of humour.

Six weeks into the journey, the worst happened. India fell in love with the second son of a foreign Count when the *Hortensia* stopped for three days at his family's vineyard-surrounded estate. In less than seventy-two hours India was wooed, proposed to, adopted into the bosom of the family, and began writing wedding invitations.

Metis had never felt so betrayed. She could have stayed with India, of course, but with a quarter of Teacup Isles society invited to the wedding, she was likely to find herself besieged by everything she was running away from. Her last crumb of freedom would disappear.

After escaping the marriage market, the last thing she wanted was to commit the next year of her life to being a professional bridesmaid.

Grimly, she waved goodbye to her friend and returned to the *Hortensia*. She could not go home, could not imagine ever being ready to go home. Still, the thought of staying on this boat, surrounded by forced manners and jolliness at all turn, *completely alone* made her want to scream.

Tonight's theme dance was 'Ocean Fantasy.' The residents of the *Hortensia* took to it with delight, festooning themselves and the upper deck of the ship with blue and green 'seaweed' ribbons, dolphin head-dresses and octopus hats.

Metis had, in the face of the enthusiasm of the captain's young and bubbly nieces, allowed herself to be talked into a bright blue wig in the court style of the last century, with a jewelled galleon atop it. She felt like a fool.

The gown was a little scandalous, showing more of her shoulders than her mamma would have liked, but if Mamma wanted a say in how Metis dressed for parties, Mamma shouldn't have got herself locked up for magical malfeasance and petty treason.

It wasn't even a good party. The usual suspects murmured to each other while nibbling on cold salmon and glazed carrots. The string quartet played the same fourteen songs they played on every occasion.

Metis stood alone, more beautiful than she had ever looked in her life, desperately lonely.

Surely it was time to write to her cousins and beg the price of passage home.

Metis had promised herself she would not return until she had circumnavigated the Continent, and found purpose in her life; now, after two months and barely a quarter of the Continental coastline, she was ready to let go of her dreams.

She might have done exactly that, if not for the mermaid.

The mermaid was golden: her hair long and curling, her body tanned and generously curved. She looked like a carved figurehead, warm and come to life. She wore a gown that would have been entirely scandalous if this was not a masquerade. It shimmered with emerald beading, hugging her body in places unheard of in Teacup Isles society, and revealing not only bare shoulders and elbows but almost her entire back, right down to her waist.

A false tail made from padded silk curled around the wide skirt of the dress. Beneath it, the mermaid's feet were bare. It was this more than anything which felt like a shock to Metis; a lady might wear all manner of questionable attire at a themed ball, but bare feet were for intimates only.

The mermaid was dancing. How she danced, spinning and whirling so that every inch of her could be seen; hair and shoulders, backless gown, bare feet, silk tail.

Every sailor gaped. Every passenger stared. And Metis… Metis could not take her eyes off this beautiful woman.

(*Oh,* she thought in a secret voice, down beneath her ribs, *is that why so many of the eligible men always seemed so very dull?*)

Most extraordinary of all, after the dance came to an end, the golden mermaid arrowed in on Metis as if she was the most fascinating person in the room, with such determination that every party guest turned to see who, exactly, had this strange creature's fascination.

Metis felt her colour rising; even in a blue wig, she was cursed with the fair and responsive skin of a redhead. Any hint of embarrassment was blazoned on her face.

"You," said the mermaid in a throaty voice. "Look like you are not having any fun." She sipped from a tankard that did not match the usual tableware of the *Hortensia*; nothing about this woman was familiar.

This was the first time Metis had met someone new since that whole business with India's sudden betrothal.

"You don't belong here," she breathed.

The mermaid quirked an eyebrow, glancing around at the stuffy party. "Neither do you, darling," she observed.

Metis could have kissed her. She could imagine nothing worse than meeting a beautiful stranger who thought she did, in fact, belong to the captain's favoured guests on the *Hortensia*.

The mermaid smiled, filling the entire deck with the glow of her approval. "Do you want to get out of here, lovey?"

Where? was a question that perhaps, Metis should have asked, but she had already guessed at the answer.

They had been berthed for two days at the coastal city of Yauncestri, which offered the *Hortensia* passengers a pleasant tour of ruins in the nearby hills, and a brief visit to the local glove museum.

During that time, a smaller ship was berthed next to them: a sturdy if ramshackle privateer named the *Caliban*.

Every time Metis glanced over the rail (from behind the lace parasol forced upon her by the captain's nieces every time she set out on deck without one) she could not help but think that everyone on the *Caliban* was having a far better time than everyone on the *Hortensia*.

The crew of the *Caliban* — there appeared to be no passengers — were a motley assortment of rogues and ruffians. They wore clashing clothes in bright colours, played music with improvised instruments and sang shanties as they worked. They all seemed to genuinely like each other, constantly exchanging friendly touches, smacks on the back, casual tousling of the hair. The men wore lace and ruffles; the women wore breeches. There were several crew-mates whose gender was not immediately apparent.

Metis had been longing to meet them all, all the while knowing it was impossible.

On the night she and her mermaid abandoned the *Hortensia* and slipped aboard the *Caliban*, they arrived in the thick of an entirely different party. This one was also masked, though the music was wilder, the lanterns burned lower, and the dancing was just short of scandalous.

"You said you wanted adventure," said the mermaid, handing Metis a skewer of grilled meat and several vegetables she did not recognise. "Welcome aboard, sweetheart."

No one knew who she was. No one knew *where* she was. It was the most thrilling thing that had ever happened to her, and Metis wanted more.

She danced, she sang, she ate meat on a stick and drank something out of a tin mug that might actually be beer.

As the night crawled towards its end, Metis found herself wedged into a corner of the quarter deck, her head resting on the pillowy bosom of a mermaid.

"Calypso!" roared a deep, commanding voice.

Metis snapped to attention, her dreamy half-awake

state disappearing as if a cold bucket of water had sluiced all over her.

A tall man stood over them both: the most extraordinary man Metis had ever beheld. This was not one of the soft-handed lords and viscounts with whom her mamma had been desperate to pair her.

He wore black leather from boot to shoulders, and he fitted it well. He had long black braids, a small black beard, and eyes that — for want of a better word — smouldered.

Had they turned out men like *these* at the garden parties, she would have been far more enthused to attend.

The mermaid woke with a slow smile, and snuggled Metis closer to her impressive bosom. "Honey," she purred.

The smouldering man growled under his breath. "Don't call me honey on deck."

"Bonny," said the mermaid, stretching her limbs. (Oh dear, Metis must have introduced herself as Bonny Blythe, how embarrassing) "May I introduce you to J. Willoughby Bones, captain of the *Caliban* and master of my heart."

Of course. Metis had just met the two most attractive and impressive people in her life, and they were in love with each other.

"Calypso," the captain growled again. "We sail at dawn. Send your ladyfriend on her way unless she wishes to join the crew."

The mermaid's face lit up with delight.

"No," said the captain sharply.

"But *honey*, we've been short-handed since Edgar and Balthazar ran off to get married," she crooned. "Sal needs an assistant, you know they do."

Metis shivered with a combination of embarrassment and… something else she did not want to identify, as the captain looked her over. She sneezed, and to her horror, the tall blue wig gave up the ghost, slipping forward over her face.

"Doesn't look much like a sailor," the captain grumbled.

"Neither was I when I started." Calypso — Metis was assuming this was the mermaid's name — smouldered right back at her captain lover, arching her back to make her beaded gown look even more spectacular (if that was at all possible). "As first mate, aren't I in charge of selecting new crew?"

Metis held her breath. It had never occurred to her that she might truly be able to stay. Suddenly she wanted nothing more.

Captain Bones' long-lashed eyes returned to her. "Soft hands. You can write? Numbers? Make lists?"

Writing correspondence for endless morning after endless morning was indeed one of Metis' skills, drilled into her by a mother obsessed with turning her into a duchess. She nodded eagerly.

His eyes narrowed as he considered the matter. "Leave a note to your people," he commanded. "I don't want to get arrested for kidnapping. Dawn, Calypso! I mean it."

He strode away along the deck. Calypso had no shame in ogling him from behind as he went.

"Far too much man for one woman," she said in a most inappropriate tone of voice. "Aren't I lucky?"

"So," said Metis, sitting up straight. "You're not a mermaid."

Calypso laughed. "Better than that, my lovely. I'm a privateer. Welcome to the *Caliban*!"

I: A MOST RECKLESS MISSIVE

My dear Mrs Seabourne,

Thank you so much for your assistance in recent weeks. I have now decided upon my future husband, and will marry him in a private ceremony.

I recognise that as queen, this will be seen as a selfish act by many, including my closest confidantes. However, I have lived every second of my life in duty to the Teacup Isles. In this, I shall follow my heart.

I have departed of my own volition for my wedding in my own privateer vessel, the Caliban, captained by the inestimable Captain J. Willoughby Bones.

It would be most convenient if you could discreetly inform the following people of my departure. Everyone else may read about it in the newspaper in due course.

- *Alfred Lord Manticore, Queen's Advisor on Magical Matters*
- *Henry Jupiter, Duke of Storm*
- *Lady Hadderine Bustledown, Mistress of the Robes*
- *Mr Octavian Swift, Queen's Consultant*

> - *Prince Sauvon of Trevental, former suitor for my hand*
> - *Comte Georges of Arunia, former suitor for my hand*
> - *Duc Rudolf of Gedos, former suitor for my hand*

With the warmest of regards and appreciation,
Aud Arabellesque Titania Montanney-Whisk
Queen of the Teacup Isles

~

It was safe to say that Mrs Mnemosyne Seabourne had never read such an upsetting and utterly *reckless* missive in her life. Given her own family's propensity for dramatic correspondence, this was saying something.

She slipped her hand into one of the pockets tied on to her dress, to check that her glass hedgehog Basil was still there. He nuzzled at her hand; she should not have brought him, of course, but when she left home two days ago, it had been in expectation of a picnic, not a series of diplomatic disasters. Basil liked a picnic. He had a particular taste for watercress sandwiches.

"Where did you find this letter?" Mneme heard her husband, Mr Thornbury Seabourne, ask Lord Manticore.

"It was left behind at the camp on Ghost Island, when her Majesty disappeared," replied Lord Manticore, clearly distressed. Hardly surprising, since his secret love for the Queen was known to everyone in the room. He crumpled and re-flattened the letter, staring at it mindlessly.

Rather presumptuous of him, as the letter was not his to destroy, but Mneme chose not to make a scene.

Not so her husband. "And you thought nothing of opening a letter addressed to my wife?" Thornbury inquired mildly.

Lord Manticore gave him a furious look. "It was a matter of national security!"

"Hush, both of you," said Mneme, reclaiming the letter in order to read it over again. When she was done, she handed it to Thornbury, trusting him to keep the parchment safe from any peers who might want to visit wanton destruction upon it. "This missive is in the Queen's hand. Can you confirm whether she wrote it of her own volition?"

Thornbury cast a few minor charms of revealing. "Legitimate," he confirmed finally.

"She could have been forced to write it at sword-point, or compelled by some act of malevolent magic," growled Lord Manticore, vibrating with barely suppressed rage. "I cannot believe her Majesty would be so reckless with her own safety. To put herself in the hands of vagabond sailors…"

There was a discreet cough in the corner, reminding them of the fourth member of their party.

Thornbury had led all four of them through the portal from Storm North to Wistworia Palace; they were now closeted in a private study with a great many suspiciously symmetrical leather-bound books on tall shelves.

Mneme had never been formally introduced to the fourth gentleman. She knew his first name was Dominic and that he was some form of Queen's man, which meant he worked in the intelligence service under the command of Mr Octavian Swift, her slightly estranged father-in-law.

This Dominic had, by all accounts, been protecting Cousin Henry from assassins for some time now, and had recently been revealed as the former brother-in-law of Henry's wife (and Mneme's friend) Juno, the new Duchess of Storm.

In any case, Mneme had been swept into an entirely

informal acquaintance with the gentleman thanks to all manner of strange events, without being aware of his full name. Thornbury referred to him as 'the Ghost' which Mneme refused to take seriously, especially considering they had been standing on Ghost Island at the time. She had once attempted to call him 'Dominic' as if he were a footman, hoping this would be insulting enough that someone might correct her.

(This backfired when it turned out Mr "the Ghost" was a cousin by marriage twice removed, making it practically appropriate to be on first name terms.)

Dominic 'the Ghost' of No Last Name was a tall man whom Mneme's mamma might have deemed 'quite presentable.' He had a solid, heroic-looking jawline and oddly pale eyes. He was, for reasons of state, still dressed all in black after impersonating Duc Rudolf of Gedos. He wore several gleaming rings bearing sinister sigils which suggested that among other things, he was a magister of high rank, with a taste for necromancy.

Mneme would have guessed that, even without the rings. Magic oozed out of his pores. She was not a qualified magister herself, her specialty being the domestic magics for which ladies did not get sent to university, but you would have to be blind and null not to sense the power in this gentleman.

Dominic was, in short, a suspicious character, and yet both Lord Manticore and Thornbury had thought nothing of including him in a sensitive private meeting about the Queen's sudden elopement.

If Mneme could ever get her husband alone, she might be able to interrogate him for details, but if the crises kept building, that might never happen again.

"Rather than waste time," said the suspicious character. "I suggest we proceed as if the letter is true. Catching the

Caliban at sea must be our first priority. If her Majesty is, as she writes, a willing participant in her flight…"

"Impossible," raged Lord Manticore.

"…then I refuse to believe that our Queen would be capable of conducting a secret romance — or secret marriage alliance — without *someone* knowing what she was up to," Dominic concluded. "One does not accept a suit out of nowhere."

"He's right," agreed Thornbury. "Storm is out of commission for this one." Henry had agreed to stay home with his pregnant wife after their recent adventures. "He was just as surprised as the rest of us, though. We should see if the Queen's Consultant knows any more." Thornbury winced, a common involuntary reaction when referring to his father.

"Do as you like," said Dominic dismissively. "It won't get you very far. If we wish to find out the Queen's recent state of mind, better to consult the Mistress of the Robes. Marriage is women's business."

Mneme glanced down at the letter again. "She is above Mr Swift on the list to be informed," she murmured.

Lady Hadderine Bustledown, Mistress of the Robes.

"Time is of the essence," Lord Manticore growled. "Who knows what's happening to the Queen on that blasted ship?"

2

BONNY BLYTHE

ONE YEAR AGO

Metis was terrified at first that she would humiliate herself on the *Caliban*: that they would all instantly recognise her as a lady playacting at being a sailor.

But facing failure was something she had done every day since her first Season out in society; she had survived it then.

This was easier. Not only because Mamma wasn't hovering around, trying to cheat and connive and encourage tiny magical 'helping hands' at every turn.

Calypso had begun by pushing Metis — or rather, Bonny Blythe, as she'd never admitted to that particular lie — into the hands of Sal, the ship's highly capable bosun.

Along with steering the ship when the captain and first mate were busy, the bosun's main job was handling supplies and stores on board. In essence, this was the job that Metis had trained for her whole life: running a household. Counting barrels and crates, negotiating with suppliers, keeping careful tallies, and managing the expectations of everyone on the crew…

Being a privateer, Metis learned, was not exactly the opposite of being a pirate: the crew were in service to the Crown, but in times of war they had royal permission to act as piratical as they liked against Queen Aud's enemies. The Teacup Isles were not currently at war, so apart from the occasional gallivant in the direction of the Troilish Empire, the *Caliban* had become a glorified courier vehicle.

Still, there were enough bright headscarves, eye-patches and cutlasses aboard to make little aesthetic difference between the two vocations. Like pirates, privateers flouted convention and laughed in the face of society's unspoken rules.

Take Sal, for instance: their bosun was a burly soul who refused to be defined by their gender, wore jewels in their beard, and swapped back and forth between breeches and petticoats as if it was of no more account than deciding between two pairs of boots.

Jacob Fry, the head gunner, was courting Sebastian Smedley, the ship's surgeon — though one of them had been born in the gutter and the other educated in the finest of schools.

Ginger, the quartermistress, wore more lip-paint than an opera singer, dyed her long hair every colour of the rainbow, and made it very clear to anyone who might be confused that however she might have been born, she was a woman now.

Lillit, Damon and Hobsbawn, a merry trio of able seamen, were in a three-way marriage that had lasted twenty years.

Rafferty, the ship's cook, had two wives (and eight children!) somewhere on shore. According to Sal, Rafferty's wives lived together in domestic harmony, which was improved greatly by having a husband who was only home a few weeks of the year.

Metis might have started out on board the *Caliban* as the most sheltered creature this crew had ever met, but she adapted quickly. The freedoms of the ship were exciting, allowing her to explore her own preferences, as tame as they might be: the greatest of her discoveries so far was how much she liked wearing trousers, especially the pair Calypso had given her with twelve patch pockets, each in a different colour.

With the assistance of Ginger, Metis dyed her hair bright blue, and wore it piled up under a black velvet cap. (She had been tempted to cut it all off like Lillit, but couldn't quite bring herself to go that far.)

Thanks to a generous clothes-swapping policy, Metis now wore bright, pretty shirts, all in hues her mamma would never have allowed — *not with your red hair, my dear, prospective husbands only wish to see young ladies in cream or white…*

Ginger wore the gown Metis had brought with her from the *Hortensia* with far more style and confidence than Metis ever could… and the wig had now been dyed pink.

Metis found herself encouraged to make all manner of small but important changes beyond her clothes and hair. She drank tea with two sugars, and ate as many cakes as she liked — which as it turned out, was not nearly as many as she had craved back when her mamma kept insisting she shouldn't eat any.

She laughed loudly instead of hiding amusement behind a paper fan. She learned to tie knots, gut fish and haul sail. She even learned to sing a few shanties along the way — even louder than she laughed. *Oh, Metis, you don't have a refined enough voice to sing in public, better to play accompaniment for the other young ladies, sitting at the piano is so flattering to the figure…*

Metis never got over her awe of the fierce, imposing

Captain Bones. He felt impossibly large and beautiful, like a character in a story. The captain never said a word to suggest she was not up to the work. He remembered her name when they passed on the deck. He looked out for his people, and that now meant Metis, too. It was intoxicating, to be part of a community like this, under a captain like that.

Bonny Blythe grew callouses on her hands. She learned how to swab a deck and hang a hammock, and she knew exactly how many tots of rum were stored on ship at any moment of the day. Astonishingly, she became an intimate friend of First Mate Calypso, who was just as beautiful and mighty and awe-inspiring as Captain Bones, but also impish, silly and warm-hearted.

"We can't be in here," Metis hissed the first time Calypso tried to drag her into the captain's cabin.

"You said you wanted tea, darling."

Tea was readily available from the galley — brewed eye-wateringly strong and served in tin cups — but the captain owned the only proper teapot on board.

"Calypso, I can live without it," Metis replied, mortified. "Don't make me go in there."

It was hard to say no to those bright green eyes, that laughing mouth. They were friends, and Metis was grateful for it — but she could not swear she was not also entirely smitten. Luckily neither Calypso nor Captain Bones were aware of her crush.

"Fine," said Calypso, pretending to be aggrieved. "You keep watch. I'll steal his tea set for you."

"Wait," said Metis. "No, that's worse!"

They ended up in the crow's nest, pouring perfectly brewed tea out of a porcelain teapot into tiny china cups with proper handles. Privateers drank tea even more than they drank rum, and they collected tea blends from all over the world. These teas were all highly spiced or flavoured: called things like Unicorn's Tears, Siren Song, or Queen of Tides.

Delicious and strange and a bit too much, just like everything else on board the *Caliban*.

Metis thought her roughened hands might make the porcelain rattle, but apparently she remembered exactly how to hold the delicate handles and saucers.

There were no cakes or muffins to go with the tea, as might have been laid at her mamma's table. Calypso had nicked some hard-as-nails treacle scones from the galley, and now broke them into dainty pieces.

"Right, then, assistant bosun Bonny Blythe," she said, bright eyes gleaming with intent. "Tell me all your secrets."

"I don't have any secrets," Metis said, sipping at Unicorn's Tears, which tasted of fruits and flowers and fresh air.

Calypso gave her a scathing look. "Do all fancy ladies lie as much as you do?"

"I'm not a fancy lady. I hated that life."

Calypso faked a swoon, which was a daring manoeuvre in the crow's nest. "*Oh no, my parents are so wealthy I own land and horses, however will I survive such torment?*"

"Are you suggesting," said Metis quietly, feeling a little put out. "That I had nothing to run away from?"

"Darling, I'd never suggest that," said Calypso, straightening up quickly and petting Metis' hair. "I wouldn't be a highborn lady if you paid me."

Metis had been about to tell Calypso her whole story. The warlock father who had abandoned her to the care of an obsessive match-making mamma. Two cousins she had resented her whole life, because of how she was constantly compared to their success.

A brief moment of madness in which the possibility of becoming the Duchess of Storm and escaping her mamma had actually let Metis think it was a solid life plan to trick one of her cousins into marriage…

Rock bottom: when Mamma used forbidden magic to abduct Cousin Henry (her own nephew!) and set herself up as his bride. Public humiliation. Criminal trial. Her mother imprisoned in the Tower of Thyme…

Now, looking into the beautiful face of her teasing, merry friend, Metis lost all will to confess her secrets.

She popped two pieces of dusty treacle scone in her mouth and instantly regretted it.

"Spit them on the deck," Calypso urged.

Her mouth was full of tar and unhappiness. "Splurgle," said Metis, worried what would happen if she accidentally spat it on to the head of a fellow sailor. Or a seagull.

"Are you a privateer or a princess?" Calypso demanded. "Spit it out, man!"

Metis spat, and they watched the dark gobbet of distress sail down and land messily but inevitably at the feet of Captain J. Willoughby Bones.

Metis almost swooned in horror.

The captain stared at his polished boots, at the splatted mess on the deck, and then finally looked up. "Calypso," he said in measured tones.

"Aye aye, honeybunch?" his first mate called down.

"Do you have my best tea service up there in the crow's nest?"

"Of course I do."

"As you were." He strode across the deck to talk to Ginger.

Calypso sighed dreamily, chin on both hands. "He's such a good man," she murmured. "I'm going to break his heart someday."

"You don't have to," said Metis, her hands tightening around the porcelain teacup in alarm.

"I know," said Calypso, and she no longer sounded like she was joking. "And, yet. Happiness is not built to last."

~

Two months later, Calypso was gone. Captain Bones got fiercely drunk and stayed that way for fourteen days straight, shut up in his cabin, roaring in rage at anyone who disturbed him.

The crew was shattered. Their latest mission was a mess, thanks to their entire leadership team being out of commission. Morale was at an all-time low… and yet. Life had to go on, somehow.

"Why me?" Metis protested as Ginger and Sal pushed her off the quarter-deck and towards her doom.

"He'll listen to you, bright eyes," said Ginger, lying shamelessly.

"He likes you," Sal agreed, adding to the lies. "He hardly ever shouts at you." That was true. Or it had been, before their world ended.

"He's just worried I'm going to turn back into a lady and cry on him," Metis grumbled. She hated getting special treatment. If the captain had ever been kinder to her than any other crew-mate, it was because of her close friendship with Calypso, which would no longer win her any favours.

Still, you couldn't argue with a vote. The privateer life involved a surprising number of formal and informal elections. If no one abided by the results, anarchy would ensue.

The tally was in, and Metis was up.

She grudgingly accepted the mug of Siren Song (brewed so strong and sweet that a teaspoon wouldn't just stand up in it, it would dance a jig) and supper plate placed in her hands by Rafferty the cook. She slouched reluctantly in the direction of the cabin down in the aft of the ship.

Metis had always liked the captain's cabin. It was rather grand, with polished wood everywhere, a mighty desk, and cozy cushions tucked into the large back windows. Like a gentleman's study, but better, because it was at sea. Everything was better at sea.

Right now, the cabin was a wreck. Drunk!Captain Bones had taken out his frustration on the soft furnishings. His hammock hung sadly from a single string. There were two cutlasses literally stuck in the inside of the door when Metis pushed it open.

"Get out!" roared the captain, rising from his chaos-strewn desk. Several pens came with him as he lurched upwards, most attached to his unkempt beard, one embedded in his face.

He had a fifth of rum left in his last bottle. Talking him down now was a safer option than waiting for his enforced sobriety.

"You have to eat something," said Metis, holding out the tin plate and mug. "Or you'll die." The Siren Song tea smelled of chocolate, and oranges, and cannon smoke.

Her captain's eyes were bloodshot, his skin clammy. He'd never looked less attractive in his life. Still rocking the leather trousers, but they lost their appeal when you realised he hadn't changed them in a week. Bones glared at Metis with what energy he had left. "Leave me alone, Blythe," he growled. "Unless you want my dagger in your…"

"Your daggers are in the ceiling," said Metis. She

glanced upward. He did have rather a lot of daggers. "Were you trying to stab the boat? It's not a good idea to put holes in the boat. That's basic captaining, I shouldn't have to explain that to you."

"If you don't get out, I'm going to make you…" Bones staggered to his feet, which was a mistake. He went down sideways, leather-clad legs tangled up with his own boots, or lack of boots. He only had a striped sock on his left foot, with a hole over the toe, which might be why he went, in a phrase Metis would never be able to say aloud no matter how many times she heard it shouted across the deck, *arse over tit*.

She put the plate and the tin mug carefully on the desk. She leaned over her sodden wreck of a captain, keeping enough of a distance to prevent herself from being knocked unconscious by the rum fumes. "How's the weather down there?" she ventured.

"Leave me to die," Bones groaned.

Metis kicked him in the shoulder. It was a gentle kick, but she had leather boots these days, and her toe was reinforced with steel.

Bones grunted, and gave her a startled look.

Metis thought about the worried faces of the crew, all the nudges and mutters and concern that had been brewing for days. *Weeks*. She thought about the fact that, in deciding who should face the captain in his den of misery, over three quarters of the crew had voted for her.

Or, at least, they had voted for Bonny Blythe…

She put her hands on her hips, channelling all the confident people she had ever known in her life — her aunts, her mamma, Cousin Henry, Cousin Mneme. (*Calypso*, she thought traitorously, and jammed that thought down under her ribs where it wouldn't hurt so much.)

"Get up, man," Metis demanded in the ringing tones

of Bonny Blythe, assistant bosun. "Have some pride. Calypso didn't just leave you, she left *us*. Your crew are trying to run this ship without our first mate or our captain. We've had three paper birds from the palace in the last forty-eight hours, and no one has the authority to even read the messages. Sal hasn't slept for two days, Fry and Smedley aren't speaking to each other, and Lillit's refusing to leave the crow's nest. Everyone is heartbroken."

I'm heartbroken, she did not say. *Calypso was my friend and I trusted her and she left me too. I have a horrible feeling she had been planning to do this long before I came aboard and I can't tell anyone, least of all you. Because I was stupidly in love with your girlfriend and I hope you never find out.*

Metis picked up the tin plate on the desk and slammed it down again, for effect. "Rafferty made you one of those pies you like, and it's not even your birthday. Get it together."

Bones gave her a weary, upside-down sad smile.

Stop that, Metis told her heart sternly, as it flipped over. *No flutters. This man is not for you.*

Bonny Blythe folded her arms, and glared at her captain until he staggered to his feet, and back into his chair. She kept glaring as he ate the pie in three bites, washed it down with the chocolatey-citrusy tea, and stared crankily into the empty tin mug as if the lack of rum offended him. "Tell Sal they're the first mate now," he muttered.

Metis threw up her hands. "That leaves us without a bosun! Those who don't starve in the first week will end up duelling each other to death over the payroll."

Captain Bones rolled his eyes at her, and shoved the empty mug back in her direction. "Don't be stupid, Blythe. You're the new bosun."

Metis had never felt such a swift transition from indignant to embarrassed. "*What?*"

The captain passed a hand over his face. "I need to shave."

"That's true enough. I've never seen a beard so untidy, and I just watched Rafferty bake a pie. I'll send Doc Smedley in to see to it if you promise not to bellow at him, he's having a hard day. *What?*" she added again, still stuck on the first thing.

Surely it was too soon for a promotion like that. Metis hadn't even been in the crew for half a year yet, and…

The captain gave a heavy sigh. "You run the numbers faster than Sal. They've been offloading most of their spreadsheets on you since you got here. Your handwriting is more legible than literally every other person on this ship, and… ugh." Bones had staggered far enough across the cabin to see at himself in the mirror, and did not like what he saw. "Crew trusts you. I trust you. Get on with it, sailor."

"Yes, cap'n," Metis said automatically. "There are three vegetables left on your plate, and you should eat them," she added, before ducking out of the door.

"Bosun Blythe," he bellowed after her.

Metis almost walked into a wall. *Bosun Blythe.* Would she feel the same giddy pride if he had called her Bosun Seabourne?

No one else in my family has ever achieved anything like this. They wouldn't know how.

"Yes, cap'n?" she said smartly, returning to the doorway.

"Nothing," Bones said with a ghost of a grin that reminded her how handsome he was, under better circumstances. "Just wanted you to hear it out loud."

Metis grinned back at him, warm and full of unbear-able happiness. "It sounds good."

II: A CAVALCADE OF CORRESPONDENCE

Thornbury assigned himself the task of informing his father about recent events. Assuming, of course, that the Queen's Consultant had not already heard about the matter of the elopement and/or abduction of Queen Aud. Swift was the type to have spies in the walls, and surveillance charms on every passing sparrow.

To Mneme's relief, Thornbury dragged Lord Manticore away with him for this particular chore. She sympathised with the man's situation in theory, given his long-suppressed (supposedly mutual) passion for the Queen, et cetera, et cetera, but after several hours in Manticore's company, Mneme had long passed the point of *literal* sympathy.

Pining for a lost love was a quality best kept to heroes in gothic novels. In real life, it was remarkably tiresome.

It was left to Mneme to break the news to Lady Hadderine Bustledown, one of Queen Aud's most elderly and reliable aunts, who ran the royal household as Mistress of the Robes.

Mneme took Dominic with her, hoping she would not

have to introduce him to anyone she knew. It would be entirely undignified to come out with "and this is Mr The Ghost" in public, but what option did she have?

This turned out not to be a problem because the Mistress of the Robes was already acquainted with the gentleman.

"Hmmph," said Lady Hadderine. Her receiving room was decorated with the wildest combination of floral patterns that Mneme had ever seen in her life, and no less than three chandeliers. Her face, creased like a raisin with age and surrounded by a fine lace bonnet, was unimpressed. "Still here, young man?"

"Making myself useful, my lady," said Dominic with a practiced bow.

Mneme handed over the letter, not sure she could trust herself to explain the situation without fluttering about. The sudden elopement of a queen did rather inspire panic, and Mneme had been working to keep hers tamped down.

Lady Hadderine, who had lived through more royal scandals than hot cups of tea, read the letter without a single flail or gasp. "My word," was all she said at first. Any further response was confined to quiet tutting.

"Do you have any idea *whom* the Queen is planning to marry?" Mneme begged.

"Other than Prince Sauvon, Comte Georges, and Duc Rudolf," Dominic put in. "Prime suspects indeed, but all accounted for on the island," he added to Mneme in an undertone.

"That doesn't narrow it down, my dears," said Lady Hadderine, getting herself rather creakily to her feet. "Have either of you ever seen the Hall of Proposals?"

~

"No," said Dominic, a few minutes later. "I believe you're right, Lady H. This does not help to narrow it down."

The Hall of Proposals was a high-ceilinged room with gilded windows, spacious enough to host a moderate country dance… if not for the giant table that filled most of the hall. The table groaned under its heavy load of gleaming, glittering gifts. Jewellery, silks, musical instruments, ornate porcelain vases, antique statues… all manner of expensive tat along with hundreds of large, gold-edged envelopes in stacks. On shelves that lined the room, buckets and buckets held thousands more letters and cards. The whole situation was on the verge of exploding into a cavalcade of correspondence.

Every item was labelled in elaborate detail. Clearly it was someone's job to keep track of all this. Several someones. An army of tactful secretaries, armed with pen and ink.

"These are just the marriage proposals sent to *our* queen?" Mneme asked. "Not — archives going back generations?"

It was less than seven years since Queen Aud's coronation.

"Our queen only," confirmed Lady Hadderine. "The items on the table consist of the proposals and related gifts she has received in the last six months."

"Go on, Mrs Seabourne," said Dominic. "Which do you think is the relevant item?"

Mneme gave him an odd look, wondering if he was making fun of her. "Excuse me?"

His sinister expression softened. "I'm not expecting miracles, but surely there's a spell…"

"Aren't *you* a magister?" she inquired. "We should wait for Lord Manticore, in any case…"

"Lord Manticore is a mess," Dominic said crisply. "I

wouldn't trust him to charm his way out of a wet paper bag right now. Your husband, Mr Thornbury — my apologies, Mr *Seabourne* — is expert in the disassembly of existing spells, and my own specialty is necromancy. Neither of which is useful in this case. Whereas I have it on good authority that you are one of the most accomplished practical authorities on sympathetic magic in the Teacup Isles. Unless you think some other form of charmwork would be more appropriate?"

That was… incredibly flattering. If she wasn't in such a flap about the Queen's surprise elopement, Mneme might have come to a similar conclusion. Sympathetic magic, *of course*. Not every problem needed to be solved with raw power. She might not be a university graduate, but she had trained under her mamma and two Seabourne aunts who between them were equivalent of high magisters in domestic magic.

Thornbury had been boasting about her. Mneme must (gently) rebuke him for it later.

"I'll need some sealing wax," she considered. "Also, string."

Sympathetic magic was small in nature. It was used to create tiny reflections of reality: magical nudges and helping hands. "*We encourage reality to match our ideal,*" her mamma used to say while folding napkins into poppets to represent everyone against whom she had ever held a grudge.

Finding stray objects was a task entirely suited to sympathetic magic. Anyone who has ever dropped a needle near a haystack or a hairpin in a ballroom knows that the only way to get it back is with a spool of thread and a knack for symbolic knot-tying.

For this particular ritual, Mneme poured a circle of wax on the polished floor, then stamped it with a seal provided by Lady Hadderine — the one used for the Queen's personal correspondence. Mneme cast a ball of string into the air before her, connected by one end to the stamped wax seal.

By the time Thornbury and Lord Manticore threw open the doors of the Hall of Proposals to join them, the spell was already underway.

The string spiralled out across the table, ducking in and out of gleaming royal courting gifts.

"Is this really —" protested Lord Manticore.

"Shh," said Thornbury, who had long been an admirer of Mneme's work. Truly, the best of husbands.

The string re-coiled itself, whirring and spinning back into a ball. Now tied to the very end of the string was an innocuous parchment scroll, addressed in bright blue ink.

There was a wax seal on the scroll — broken — featuring three gold seashells. Mneme did not recognise the seal, which was odd; after years of being harassed to find a husband by a match-making mamma, she was acquainted with most of the noble families of the Teacup Isles, and many beyond their shores.

Lord Manticore made a strangled sound. "The Queen," he gasped when he could finally breathe. "She has been wearing a bracelet since the summer, with a gold seashell upon it."

Thornbury looked pained, as if he was getting one of his headaches right between the eyes.

Dominic the Ghost began to laugh.

Mneme was deeply irritated by all three of them. "Gentlemen," she said crisply. "If you know something, please do not be coy."

"I know which family that seal belongs to," said Thornbury. "If their island is where Queen Aud has gone…"

"It doesn't exist," interrupted Lord Manticore. "It can't exist."

"… then I'm not sure we can get her back," Thornbury completed his sentence.

A pall fell upon the room.

Finally, Dominic said: "We're going to need a boat."

3

SEAL OF SEASHELLS BY THE SEASHORE

Miss Metis Seabourne did not grow up in a fine country estate like her cousins. Her mamma, Mrs Hekate Seabourne, disliked the outdoors, and her father, Mr Gaulliver Seabourne, disliked the ocean. This was somewhat limiting, when one resided in a kingdom of islands, but they managed.

They lived in a townhouse in the most central region of the Isle of Memory, in the city of Solstice, famous for two magical universities, seven libraries, and at least fourteen geographic curses.

(The Seabourne family were not responsible for *all* the curses in the city, but Metis knew her mamma had personally cast at least six).

She was four years old when her parents stopped speaking to each other. She never knew why. Her childhood became littered with passive aggressive notes and long, awkward silences in every room of the house.

An only child, she was charged with the role of messenger pigeon, carrying word from her mother's magical studio in the attic to her father's magical studio in the cellar, not to mention all the messages required for the servants in the kitchen, and the suppliers of magical ingredients.

Sometimes they didn't even bother to ask, simply stuck a note to her jumper or worst of all, waved a silent charm at her, compelling her to march into a particular room of the house and recite the instructions from one parent to the other.

The only time Metis felt like she could breathe and be herself instead of an awkward adjunct to her parents' failed marriage was when she could smell the sea air. This meant a visit to one of the family estates — Shellwich Standing, hosted by Aunt Galatea, or Storm North, hosted by Aunt Antiope.

When she was ten years old, Metis' father disappeared, suddenly and without notice. Gaulliver Seabourne's cellar studio was left empty, swept clean of all trace of him, as if he had never existed.

"Never mind that man," said her mother. "Find me those volumes of botanical spells I was talking about the other day. And tell Sadie to drop kedgeree off our breakfast menu. No one else likes it."

Love could hardly be something Metis had romantic notions about, with a family like hers. Her aunts' husbands did not run away, but no one in the family had the kind of relationship that one wrote sonnets about.

Mamma often commented bitterly that the only point of marriage was to improve status — as her sister Antiope had done, in landing the Duke of Storm.

The society marriage market was a game played only by the gentry, in which the prize was a wedding (dull) and independence from one's family (promising). Only after her whole family collapsed into scandal and despair after her mother's recent crime did Metis truly realise what an empty dream it was. Hardly even a dream. A survival plan, highly flawed, and impossible to execute to any degree of satisfaction.

Her next escape plan turned out rather better. Metis gladly leaped from the Teacup Isles to the *Hortensia*, and from the *Hortensia* to the *Caliban*. Now her home was the ocean, the sky. Every minute of every day felt like freedom. Even when the work was hard. Even when her knuckles dried out and cracked. Even when she awoke in a swinging hammock in the midst of a storm.

Metis never felt homesick when she poked at the memories of her old life. Only numb. She could not believe she had ever been that person, *had ever been so unhappy*, and had survived it.

Calypso and Captain Bones had proved to her that a couple could be genuinely loving and equal. Status meant nothing to the two of them — he was the captain, of course, but this never caused any particular friction. He gave Calypso orders, and she accepted them. When she genuinely thought he was wrong, she yelled at him, but it was the kind of yelling that was fond, not cruel.

(Fights always ended with the two of them disappearing into the captain's cabin together. When they returned, they had decided which of them was right, and the other showed no ill will about it.)

When Calypso left so suddenly, so cruelly, abandoning the captain and the ship, Metis got caught up in trying to help everyone else. She had little time to think through her own feelings, except in her hammock at night.

She could not be sure if the waves of betrayal and heart-sickness she felt were because of her secret romantic attachments… or because she had believed so *completely* in the relationship between Captain Bones and his first mate.

They hadn't been like her parents at all. And yet…

Calypso had abandoned their crew, as swiftly and silently and suddenly as Metis' father had left his family.

The only difference was that instead of Mamma pretending it was not hurtful for her husband to have vanished… there was the wreck of Captain Bones, mourning Calypso's loss.

The crew mourned, too. Metis didn't have to hide her misery, not when the entire crew of the *Caliban* were so cut up about half of their leadership team abandoning the other.

Work helped. Missions from the palace came in, thick and strong. They rescued the shipwrecked crew of the *Illyria* from the Charybdis Hotel in the Tourmaline Strait (surviving a near-miss with a sea serpent), they delivered a stranded secret agent from one end of the Continent to the other, and they took fire from a rogue Troilish galleon at the edge of the Lyric Sea.

Captain Bones still drank too much, but he was less of an arse about it. After that first terrible fort-night, he did not neglect his duties again. Whenever he drifted back in the direction of self-pity, Sal or Ginger would point Bosun Blythe in his general direction, and that would be enough to nudge him back on track.

The crew survived, and recovered. Months passed. It was starting to feel like losing Calypso had not been the end of the world.

Back on the *Hortensia*, Metis had written very few letters home; after she moved to the *Caliban,* she stopped writing altogether. She could not imagine how to communicate with her cousins without telling them a pack of lies. Somehow, she was not ready to let Cousin Mneme or Cousin

Henry (or Aunt Galatea, or Mamma!) know the truth about her new life.

Besides, ink was at a premium on board ship; she had to invent her own short-hand for supply notes and the ledgers, leaving out all extraneous vowels and as many consonants as possible to eke out her supplies.

That was an excuse, of course, but Metis hated the idea of having to explain her situation. To justify her choices. She was happy and well in ways that would have made no sense to her former self. How could her cousins possibly understand how much she had changed?

Mneme's letters arrived from time to time, folded into magical paper birds. They were much-delayed, but not unwelcome missives, packed with news such as Mneme's betrothal to the spellcracker Mr Thornbury, her imminent wedding plans, and her hopes that Metis would return for said wedding.

Henry wrote letters too, scribbled on family notepaper. At first these were friendly enquiries, all *what ho! hope you're having a jolly time!* After that, he began to sound all solemn and pompous, like he had been attending classes on how to sound like a Duke. Head of the family. *Patriarch*, as if a family full of magical Seabourne women needed such a thing.

Henry's letters now concluded with a stiff entreaty to let them know her location, and to reassure them that she was in good health.

You're not my captain, Metis found herself thinking resentfully, when she received one particularly polite letter offering to transfer funds if she needed them to return home.

She had been home, if home meant the Teacup Isles, half a dozen times already, whenever it was necessary for the *Caliban* to dock on home soil. The Duke of Storm didn't need to know about it.

Metis had been quite discomfited the first time that the *Caliban* brought her back to familiar waters. She no longer looked anything like the shy, tomboyish creature in sprigged muslin who fled these shores less than a year ago, but she still she fretted that the second she set foot on the docks on the Isle of Town, or Storm or Memory, she might be spotted by someone who knew her.

It didn't happen. After a while, she stopped glancing behind every corner when ashore, trusting in her bright blue hair, breeches and swaggering stance (a side-effect of living at sea for so long) to protect her from being recognised as Miss Metis Seabourne.

Now it was the end of summer. The *Caliban's* current mission was to transport Lord Manticore's worldly goods from his family estate on the Isle of Manticore to the docks of the Isle of Town, so that he could take up a now permanent living situation at Wistworia Palace.

(This had come about because of Lord Manticore's very public divorce, a news event so significant and infamous that Metis had read all about it in the Continental papers long before her cousin's letter arrived — which was entirely lacking in juicy detail even though Mneme had apparently spent her own honeymoon in the company of the former Lady Manticore.)

Metis was not especially keen on Lord Manticore, from what little she had seen at assemblies during her first Season, and more recently during their job as his personal removal company. Manticore was a tall, dark and glowering type of gentleman in a way that was wholly unattractive, despite Metis feeling quite positive about those features when embodied in Captain Bones.

The Queen was evidently fond of Lord M, or she would not have given him free use of the *Caliban*. Whether that meant there was truth in the rumour that the Queen and Lord Manticore were romantically entangled remained to be seen. Metis was no gossip, but most of the crew had been raking royal muck for weeks. Rafferty, it turned out, knew all kinds of scandalous stories going back several monarchs.

The crew were allowed a few hours of shore leave once the crates and trunks of Lord Manticore were securely stored in the hold. Metis was dragged by Lillit and Ginger into a charmingly theatrical cider house with port-hole windows ("reminds all the sailors of home!") for some serious drinking. As they stumbled back to the ship, a thick fog came up quickly. Metis found herself quite alone in it, separated from her friends.

When she heard soft footsteps on the wooden planks of the dock behind her, she called out "Lillit?" (It wasn't Ginger; Metis would have heard her high-heeled boots clacking a mile off.)

"No," said a melodic voice. "Not Ginger."

Metis turned. Her heart flipped over in the same moment. She knew that voice. "Calypso?" she breathed.

Her mermaid stepped out of the greenish-grey fog, wreathed in an eerie light that couldn't be from the low-burning gas lamps along the dock; the fog had got the better of them hours ago, swallowing every mote of visible light. "Bonny Blythe," said Calypso, and there was a warmth there, for a moment, in her bright green eyes. "My darling. I'm so glad to see you. I need your help."

"My help," Metis repeated. Shock gave way to anger. "You left us. You didn't say goodbye. The only reason we knew you hadn't been kidnapped or eaten by a kraken was because your note literally said 'Don't follow me. I haven't been kidnapped. I won't be back.' You broke our captain's heart." *And mine*, she did not say. "We were friends," she added petulantly.

"I'm sorry," said Calypso, looking ethereal, her golden hair longer than ever, wreathed in the silvery fog. "I really am, Bonny. I had no choice."

How could she have become more beautiful in her absence? That was just unfair.

"You could have explained," Metis said.

"I really couldn't. It was a —" Calypso winced, looking vulnerable for a rare moment. "Family emergency," she admitted.

Metis knew how much weight could be contained within those words.

"And that meant abandoning the *Caliban* forever, without telling us why?"

"Yes. Yes, it did."

"We would have understood."

Calypso shook her head, tears glistening in her deep green eyes. "Not everyone can discard family obligations as lightly as you, honeybunch."

Fury burned in Metis' chest. For the first time, it occurred to her that Calypso might have seen through her from the start. A spinster who ran away to sea, what a joke.

(Metis barely even used her magic any more, except when she let it bleed out of her skin to tie sail knots extra tight, or to add seaworthy strength to the ship's hull. The *Caliban* would spring a leak over her dead body, and the magic had to go somewhere now she wasn't using it to keep tea hot, or try to catch a husband.)

Metis was so busy being furious at Calypso, she was not ready to be hugged. Her friend smelled like an armful of salt water and lilies. When Calypso turned her face into Metis' neck, Metis felt herself melting into the embrace. She had missed her so much.

"Bonny Blythe," breathed Calypso, her lips brushing Metis' ear. "I ask this boon."

Metis felt a shiver go through her. She knew the sensation at once. This was not a symptom of the lovelorn. No, it was a different shiver. It was the reaction to someone casting a spell on her.

She had never told Calypso the details of her family history. Of a childhood caught between two warring magisters. Left alone with a mother who thought nothing of a little light sympathetic magic here and there, to make her daughter behave exactly as she required.

By the time Metis was sixteen, she had developed strong shielding abilities for minor charms and hexes, though she continued to do whatever Mamma asked of her. She was too much of a coward to show her hand, to reveal that she had defences.

Her skin and her soul had hardened to magical influence, over the years. Perhaps that was why she had not entirely collapsed when Mamma's treachery against the family was revealed.

I am weathered, Metis thought now. *No one's getting through my hull.*

Perhaps it was that strength, those well-honed shielding techniques that saved her now. Or perhaps it was that Calypso anchored her spell to what she believed was Metis' real name.

Whatever the reason, when Calypso commanded Bonny Blythe with her magical charmed voice to take the small golden seashell she pressed into her hand, and give it to Captain Bones when she next set eyes upon him…

Metis knew she would do nothing of the sort.

～

"Bosun, z'that you?" called a familiar voice in the fog, a while later. Sal.

"I'm here," said Metis, struggling forward, both hands in front of her. "Did Lillit and Ginger make it back?"

"Of course they did, ya lummox. You're the one we've been worried about!"

Metis took careful steps with arms outstretched, not wanting to break her nose on the side of the ship, or lose her step and plunge into the harbour. She hit something warm. Her face mashed into a thick, knitted jumper that smelled of oranges and chocolate. A pair of large hands closed around hers, holding her steady.

"There you are," said the deep, comforting voice of Captain Bones.

"Mmph," said Metis, wrapped in a surprise collision that was almost a hug. She tried to step back, out of the circle of his arms.

"Careful," Bones said, hands on her elbows. "Don't want to fall into the drink."

"That would be bad," Metis agreed dizzily. He, or at least, his jumper, had been in the presence of someone smoking pipe tobacco. It smelled horribly delicious.

Her palm clenched tightly around the golden seashell, hard enough to hurt.

"How much cider did those wretches give you?" Captain Bones sounded worried.

"I think," said Metis, and then trailed off, not sure where to go next. She felt foggy all the way through, as if the sea mist hung heavy in her lungs. What happened if you breathed in too much fog? Should she ask the ship's surgeon? "I have a message for you."

"Hang on," said Bones. His hands were still on her,

guiding her safely up the gangplank. Touching her, every step of the way, in a way that was both respectful and extremely comforting.

It was completely terrible how much Metis was enjoying his hands all over her. Even more terrible was how wretched she felt once they were safely on the deck, and he moved to a more appropriate distance.

When you next set eyes upon Captain Bones, a voice spoke in her head.

Charm. She'd been charmed. Metis remembered that, remembered fighting it. Who had cast the charm on her? (Green eyes.)

Ha. What kind of idiot thought they could cast such a minor command charm on a Seabourne woman?

Give the shell directly into his hands.

She hadn't seen him yet, had she? Not in this cloudy soup of a sea fog. She had felt him, heard him, smelled him. Almost drowned in him.

(It was embarrassing, how much she wanted him.)

Fight this. She could fight this.

"Where's Doc?" she heard the captain call to Sal. "Get him to look Blythe over. And light the warding lamps, or some bugger's going to crash into us."

"No!" said Metis, closing her eyes tightly. "Don't light them yet! I have… I have to…"

I have to protect him.

But from what?

She wished she could remember.

Ship's surgeon was an important job. The title was old, stemming from the days when magic was considered unlucky to sailors — and yet it was essential to have a magic-worker onboard, given the magic levels commonly found in the waters around the Teacup Isles. The compromise was to give your hired magister a title that suggested they were there merely to sew up minor wounds, and apply quantities of rum, tea or cloves to other ailments.

Along with basic doctoring, the ship's surgeon was responsible for casting essential magics against threats from the ocean, removing all hexes, charms and other unwanted magics from the crew (which happened more often than not, especially in the parts of the sea where sirens and sea witches were rife).

On smaller ships, the ship's surgeon also ran the galley.

Dr Sebastian Smedley, surgeon of the *Caliban*, was a handsome devil. He had long amber hair bound up tightly in a coiled braid at the back of his neck. Most days, he displayed more lace on his jacket than any of the petticoat-wearers on board. He had four gold rings dangling from each ear. His moustache not only had handlebars, but little twirls on each side, like one of those fancy purveyors of coffee you found cities along the Continental coast.

He wore a monocle, which had to be ornamental rather than functional, because his eyesight was perfect.

"Gracious," Smedley said as Metis slammed into his tiny sickbay, a cabin referred to by the rest of the crew as the Scurvy Hole thanks to its recent bright orange-and-yellow paint job. "You all right there, Bosun?"

Metis, still with her hand over her eyes, shook her head wildly.

"Hexed, I suppose," Smedley said, getting to his feet. "Or a minor curse. This happens every time we have shore leave on the Isle of Manticore. Can't talk about it?"

She shook her head.

"Blythe," called Captain Bones from right outside the door. "Are you all right?" A man who could not take a hint.

Metis separated her fingers just enough to give Dr Smedley a pleading look. She was allowed to look at *him*, after all.

"Ah," said Smedley. "Rack off, Cap'n!" he yelled through the door.

"Doc," Bones said in a growl.

"Leave me with my patient, you ass!"

Captain Bones was nothing if not considerate of the chain of command — captain did *not* trump surgeon in matters medical or magical. He grumbled about it, but he left.

The charm rose up again, sticky in Metis' throat. It was stronger than she had first imagined when — *Calypso*, she remembered suddenly, bile filling her mouth. Calypso had charmed her. To do something Metis did not want to do…

Her body convulsed. Doc Smedley, with many years of training, had a bucket in front of her just in time for her to cast up her accounts without making a mess of herself.

"A powerful compulsion charm," he said, peering through the monocle… oh, that was what it was for. Not vanity, after all. A tool for recognising spells. "Grounded in sympathetic magic, of all things. Is there some token, some item that represents the caster?"

Metis clamped her hand even tighter around the gold seashell, even as she shook her head.

"Hmm," said the surgeon, considering. "Hold this, Bosun." He pushed a bottle of rum into Metis' hand. "Look to the left porthole, if you please."

The spell didn't fight her. Metis obeyed.

Smedley's hand closed over her mouth, padded with something that smelled of… roses?

She fell into darkness, fighting the whole way.

Don't let me hurt him.

~

When Metis awoke, she was free of the curse. She knew it immediately — her head was clear, if sore. She lay flat on the tiny bunk in the corner of the Scurvy Hole, staring at a tangerine ceiling that rocked back and forth only slightly. They were still in harbour.

Doc Smedley perched on a stool nearby, reading a tea-stained journal. "You're awake," he said cheerfully. "Good news and bad news, Bosun Blythe."

Metis frowned at him.

Smedley didn't glance up from his book.

"Good news is, I located the source of the unfriendly charm, and destroyed it. I must say, your powers of magical resistance are excellent. Worthy of a spellcracker. I'd take you on as a surgical assistant in a heartbeat if I didn't think the captain would murder me for stealing his boatswain."

"And the bad news?"

Smedley's elegantly sculpted moustache twitched. "The charm left a mark."

Metis glanced down. The golden seashell was no longer in her hand, but the shape of it was branded on her palm in a purplish bruise, like someone had mistaken her for a pool of sealing wax.

"You might be stuck with it, I'm afraid. It won't heal better than that," went on the surgeon. "I could cover it with a tattoo, if you like. A crab, perhaps, or some kind of seaweed arrangement. I've been practicing with the needles in my quiet hours."

"No, thanks," said Metis, gazing at the seashell seal. "I want to remember the story behind this one."

Even if she could never tell anyone what it meant.

Calypso, what have you done?

When Metis returned to the deck, the warding lamps were lit so that the crew could see something of what they were doing despite the thick fog, wrapped around them like several smoke-infused jumpers. *Don't look*, was Metis' first thought, before remembering it was safe to do so. She surveyed the ship quickly, locating Captain Bones deep in discussion with Ginger on the quarter-deck.

His jumper was mossy green, hand-knitted in thick yarn. This was, if possible, a far more devastating look on him than the black leather.

Bones glanced in her direction. Metis nodded swiftly, to let him know she was fine. His shoulders relaxed a little, *as if he had been worried*, and he turned back to Ginger.

It was possible that Metis had simply prevented the delivery of a love letter from an old flame. But she was a Seabourne, the daughter of two of the most powerful magisters in the Teacup Isles, and she had to trust her instincts.

Someone had nefarious plans for their captain, and they thought they could use Calypso to get to him. They thought they could use *Metis*.

They would have to try harder than that.

III: A DEEPLY DISTRESSING DESTINATION

The royal rescue party, consisting of Mr & Mrs Seabourne, Alfred Lord Manticore, Dominic "the Ghost" of No Last Name, and Lady Hadderine Bustledown, travelled from one end of the Teacup Isles to the other by portal, emerging on the Isle of Nemesis. From there, they boarded another of the Queen's privateer ships: the *Rosalind*.

Captain Elizah Bell of the *Rosalind*, an elderly sailor with waist-length grey hair, muscles like knotted rope and a wardrobe entirely consisting of leather and silver skulls, laughed herself sick when she heard which ship they were chasing. "Bones? He left Ghost Island when? You'll never catch the *Caliban* in this wind." She cackled at the very thought of it. "But that handsome bastard owes me forty crowns from a bet we made last spring, so I'll give it the old sea-hag try."

The year was drawing in to the less welcoming half of autumn, and the weather was a worry. From the deck of the *Rosalind*, it felt as if there were storms lurking on every horizon, metaphorical or otherwise.

It was the wrong end of October, tipping into

November. Queen Aud should be on the Isle of Town, for the formal opening of the Season and the Court of Lords. She should, if recent attempts at international diplomacy had come off as planned, be about to announce an impending royal wedding.

None of them had seen this elopement coming. Mneme had only become a favourite of Queen Aud over the last few months, and held no official position within her household, court or service. Still, she had spent many hours in her Majesty's company since the summer.

She should have realised something was wrong. Shouldn't she?

"Where exactly are we heading?" Mneme asked her husband. Thornbury had spent a long time in consultation with Captain Bell, who continued to insist their voyage was fool-hardy. She had laughed in his face at one point of their conversation, which was not exactly promising.

Thornbury now draped an oilskin coat over Mneme's shoulders, which matched one he wore. It was heavy, lined with charms that instantly cut down the icy chill. "Have you ever heard of the Isle of Dream?" he asked.

Mneme had recently drunk an excellent cup of tea flavoured with spices and bergamot which the crew of the *Rosalind* referred to as Queen of Tides. If she had been still sipping it, she would have spat out a mouthful and thrown her whole teacup overboard. "*Excuse me?*"

"I imagine there was more swearing when you said that to the captain," remarked Dominic, appearing at Mneme's other side.

"The Isle of Dream," Mneme sputtered. "It doesn't exist outside of children's story books and pantomimes." The Teacup Isles consisted of twelve distinct island fiefdoms: Storm, Memory, Peacock, Thyme, Sandwich, Sensibility, Dormouse, Glass, Manticore, Town, Bath, and Nemesis.

There were other islands dotted here and there, of course, mostly too small, politically insignificant or secret to be included on maps: Mneme had recently become quite acquainted with a sinister little clump of rocks known as Ghost Island, and had not been charmed by it in the least.

But the Isle of Dream? Really?

"How are we supposed to find it?" she demanded. "Sail between two rainbows? Ask a passing sphinx for directions? Harness a narwhal while reciting vintage poetry?"

"The seal on that proposal contained an invitation," Thornbury said quietly. "Its intent was that it could only be used by Queen Aud, but it was never used. Now I've cracked the enchantment open, we should be able to use it to guide our ship to the same destination as the *Caliban*."

The *Caliban*. A privateer ship full of a wild assortment of eccentric characters, including (Mneme had recently learned) her own runaway cousin, who was supposed to be off somewhere on a Continental Grand Tour, not wearing trousers and kidnapping queens. *Metis, what have you got yourself into?*

She thought of something else. "How does Queen Aud know where she's going if she didn't use the invitation?"

"They must have got to her some other way. The bracelet that Manticore noticed, perhaps. Or someone delivered a new invitation in person."

It all sounded most sinister. Mneme shivered. Even with the comforting weight of the charmed oilskin over her shoulders, she felt chilled to the bone. "Isn't the Isle of Dream supposed to be all mermaids and rainbows and sweetness?"

"Depends on which stories you read," said Dominic

thoughtfully. "Sea witches, krakens and pirates feature in those stories too."

"We'll need to be prepared for anything," said Thornbury. "But, uh." He looked faintly embarrassed. "You might not be too far off with the rainbow, my dear." He nodded ahead of the ship.

On the horizon, between several wild grey sea-storms, Mneme could see one spot where the clouds parted, two impossibly bright and clear rainbow arches bursting forth.

Sea witches, krakens and pirates.

"Oh, my," she said under her breath.

4

THE MATTER OF GHOST ISLAND

The Matter of Ghost Island began with crates of teacups and tiny cakes, and ended in chaos, a storm at sea, and the end of the world.

Delivering all the components of a diplomatic tea party to a secret royal picnic was a mission so slight and insignificant that it was almost insulting; except that the crew of the *Caliban* were exhausted after several back to back swashbuckling adventures. Since that business of Lord Manticore's furnishings (nearly stolen twice thanks to pirate raids), they had rescued a kidnapped contessa, transported three cursed archaeologists from one end of the Continent to the other, and almost lost their hull to a walrus with something to prove.

In announcing this mission to the crew, Captain Bones made it very clear that supplying a few crates of enchanted flatware and cucumber sandwiches to Queen Aud on an island too tiny to appear on the map was almost as good as a holiday.

The two days that followed made it very clear that he had no idea how holidays worked.

55

A more comprehensive account is documented else-where for the reader's convenience.* For the sake of brevity, we shall summarise the most salient points as they happened to Metis Seabourne, AKA Bosun Bonny Blythe of the *Caliban*.

ITEM THE FIRST: THE DUCHESS OF STORM

Of all the random family members that Metis might have accidentally run into at Crownport, one of the busiest dockland areas of the Isle of Town, she was certainly not expecting a heavily pregnant Juno, the new Duchess of Storm.

Metis had been rather intimidated by the older woman during the business of courting the duke, and later rescuing the duke, of which the least said the better.

She had, with Cousin Mneme, attended Juno's wedding to Cousin Henry, throwing the rice and so on, shortly before taking to the ocean to escape the humiliation of being the daughter of Mrs Hekate Seabourne, traitress and criminal.

It was beyond strange to have anyone who knew Metis from her old life see her here — a blue-haired Bosun on a privateer rig, as far as it was possible to get from teagowns and croquet. Juno was respectful about the whole thing despite her evident surprise.

This awkward interaction with Metis' new cousin-by-marriage would have been perfectly tolerable were it not for:

---

* See: *Have Spirit, Will Duchess*.

ITEM THE SECOND: THE WIDOW BONES

Juno, it seemed, had a secret life, and so did Captain Bones. The two of them circled each other with enough pained tension to fill a five-act melodrama. Within the hour, the captain had lightly kidnapped the duchess. For some unaccountable reason he saw fit to bring her along on their tea party mission, introducing her to the crew as his widowed sister, two utterly confusing facts that filled Metis' head for the entire journey to:

ITEM THE THIRD: GHOST ISLAND

Why Queen Aud should wish to hold a private picnic on such a gruesome, out-of-the-way knob of rocks as Ghost Island was yet another mystery to add to this very strange day. As it turned out, the picnic was a cover for Something Political, a direct quote from Sal once the sails of the foreign ships became evident.

The foreign ships involved in the 'picnic' included a royal flagship and two support vessels each from three different Continental countries: Arunia, Gedos and Trevental. Trouble, in other words. So much trouble. Which probably explained the presence of:

ITEM THE FOURTH: THE DUKE OF STORM

Of the family members Metis most wished to avoid, Henry ranked just below her own mamma and Aunt Galatea, especially since his recent letters sounded like he was one ducal lecture away from marrying her off to a random stick-insect in a cravat.

Metis did a decent job of avoiding him, as the crates of teacups and tiny cakes were unloaded on the island, until

Juno got herself kidnapped by a creepy pale-eyed necromancer. Metis was then forced to reveal herself to Henry *in front of Captain Bones* in order to organise a hasty rescue mission.

All was well that ended well. Metis stayed out of Henry's way by taking Ginger's night watch on the *Caliban* and spending most of it tucked into the crow's nest.

This meant she got an excellent view and was able to raise the alarm when:

ITEM THE FIFTH: THE *MAJESTIC HARVEST*

Queen Aud's own flagship was attacked by flaming arrows during the last watch, just before dawn. Most of the crew of the *Caliban* tumbled out to aid with the rescue effort for the burning ship.

Ordered by her captain to stay at her post, Metis could only watch in horror as Henry threw himself into danger to rescue the passengers and crew of the *Majestic Harvest*, and her other cousin Mneme was pulled from the water.

Alive, thank goodness. Alive, well, and apparently a lady-in-waiting now. There were no fatalities. The rescued royal court were taken safely to dry land and shuffled off into the trees, where Metis could no longer keep an eye on any stray member of her family.

That was Day One. Day Two went slower, by comparison. Half the crew hung around on the *Caliban*, waiting for orders. Eventually, their crew-mates drifted back in dribs and drabs, as ordered by Captain Bones. He remained on Ghost Island for some time. Sal was one of the last to return, grumbling that the *Caliban* crew were to ready themselves for imminent departure. Further information had still not arrived by luncheon, leaving the crew with little to do but lounge around, drinking and swapping stories, finally taking a small piece of the holiday they had been promised.

Metis, freed from further family reunions, chose to swab the deck. A bit of good swabbing would calm her down nicely. Technically as a bosun she was supposed to pass that sort of job to the deckhands, but the good thing about being bosun was that everyone assumed she had a good reason for whatever she did.

(Her palm was burning, Metis realised as she closed her palms around the handle of her favourite mop. She didn't have to look to see it was the hand that still bore the purplish outline of the seashell seal.)

Bones returned in the mid-afternoon, looking exhausted. He was sober, at least, and had not brought the Duchess of Storm back with him — so Metis could be grateful for small mercies.

Climbing aboard, his face creased into a tiny smile when the first thing he saw was Metis and her mop. "Do you never take a break, bosun?"

"Wouldn't know what to do with one, captain," she replied softly.

"Cap'n," called Sal, their voice ringing all the way across the ship. When Sal got loud, it meant all attempts to resolve an issue quietly had been tried. "Can we talk about the—"

"I'm getting to it," snapped Captain Bones, sprawling on the quarter-deck, his eyes half-closed and his long leather-clad limbs spread out like a beached octopus. His shirt, black silk, was open an extra button or two, under his leather coat. He always wore black when they were due on shore; kept his colourful silks for when they were at sea.

Metis wondered when he had last slept. She did not have to wonder when he had last bathed — too long ago, was the answer, if one didn't count the recent dunking in salt water from the sea rescue in the early hours of this morning.

"You said to ready the ship for departure," Sal went on, voice still loud, inviting an audience as they strode around him, boots thudding on the deck. "We've *been* ready, but I need the destination to prepare the relevant maps and plot the course."

"I don't know our destination," growled Bones, not opening his eyes. "Her Majesty has asked us to stand by. So we stand by. You remember how standing by works, Sal? It means stop talking to me."

There was a splash nearby. A deep splash, like something had been dropped overboard. Metis wandered casually along the starboard side, and peered over. What she saw was so startling, she almost tipped forward into the drink.

Calypso stared back at her.

Their former first mate was submerged in the shallow water, bare-shouldered, her golden hair floating around her in wild, salt-drenched curls for all the world as if she was an actual mermaid.

There was a shell comb in Calypso's hair, and a decorative wad of seaweed on the other side. Had her eyes always been that green?

(*Emeralds in the fog, oh yes they had.*)

"What are you doing down there?" Metis hissed, leaning over in the hope no one else would hear her.

Calypso made a splashing gesture with her hand that was clearly intended to mean 'get down here.' You learned to follow non-verbal instructions onboard; there was so much shouting on a daily basis that someone was always nursing a sore throat.

Metis glanced around. Most of the crew had made themselves scarce thanks to the bickerfest between Bones and Sal. The captain was napping, or pretending to nap so Sal would stop harassing him. No one paid Metis any attention at all.

She went over the side, clambering nimbly down the nearest rope ladder. She'd always thought Mamma was wasting her time, insisting Metis practice her dancing skills every day from the age of three: she was not only expected to memorise the latest complex dance steps every season, but those that had been fashionable in earlier generations too. All that leaping and twirling had left this particular young lady with flexible joints, odd-shaped feet, and a sturdy pair of ankles that she put to great use in the day-to-day operations of the *Caliban*.

The seashell scar on Metis' palm twinged as she reached the foot of the ladder, but that was nothing new. She was constantly aware of it; thank goodness she had managed to conceal it with a leather half-glove so no one but Doc Smedley knew it was there.

"What are you playing at?" Metis demanded in an angry whisper, hovering on the ladder just above the water. "Why are you here?"

"Bonny," breathed Calypso, her green eyes especially large and tragic. "You're going to have to trust me."

"Trust you?" Metis shot back. "First you abandoned us without any explanation, and then when I saw you again, *you hexed me.*"

"Oh," said Calypso, startled. "You know about that."

"Yes, I know about that. I come from a magical family, which you'd know if you'd ever paid me the slightest bit of attention." That was unfair, but it was hard now for Metis to stifle her fury.

"I didn't have a choice," said Calypso. She coughed, as if saying the words made her throat close up. "I never meant to hurt you, or Bones."

"Really?" Metis said furiously. "What's this, some marvellous new skin treatment?" She tugged off the glove and stuck her hand out, palm-first, to show Calypso the mark she had left upon her.

Calypso paled. "Where did you — Bonny, what happened to the shell?"

Metis swung up a rung on the ladder, distancing herself as best she could. "Doc Smedley destroyed it," she said flatly. "You can't get to the captain through me. Don't try it again."

Calypso let out a strangled cry. "Why do you have to keep messing things up?"

"*Me?*" Metis said disbelievingly. "Wait, where are you going?"

To her astonishment, Calypso sank entirely under the water, vanishing from sight. As Metis peered down into the water, something large and green flashed at her for a moment. A tail, a huge fishy tail, bright teal and green scales gleaming wet in the sunlight, and then… gone, beneath the water.

So.

Calypso really was a mermaid.

That was.

Metis was going to have to take a moment to think about this.

And then she was going to have to talk to the captain. She couldn't keep hiding this from him.

❧

When Metis climbed back over the side, the quarter-deck was empty except for Sal, who was passive-aggressively thumbing through a stack of maps. No sign of Captain Bones.

When Metis asked where the captain was, Sal shrugged. "How should I know? Off to secret business with the queen on that bleeding island, while the rest of us hang around plaiting daisies into our beards."

It was mid-afternoon by the time Captain Bones returned to the *Caliban*. He was accompanied by a hooded, masked woman whom he escorted directly to his cabin.

The crew drifted back on to deck in order to more efficiently place bets as to who that woman was.

"The Duchess of Storm again," reckoned Damon.

"Nah, not round enough."

"It's the queen," guessed Hobsbawn.

"Her shoes looked royal," agreed Ginger with an air of authority.

"Would her Maj go anywhere without like, three maids and a butler?" mused Lillit.

"That's why she's in disguise, obviously," scoffed Ginger.

"Unless he's kidnapped her," suggested Damon, who was promptly sat on by about five people to shut him up.

The crew's spirits were cheered considerably, as if the indignity of a teacup-delivering mission turned diplomatic disaster was made up for in spades, with a secret queen-smuggling operation ahead of them.

"You look glum, chum," said Lillit, when she noticed that Metis wasn't joining in on the speculation. She was a small woman, wiry and baby-faced despite being (at last count) nearly forty. She always took pains to keep an eye out on the younger ones. "Don't *you* think it's the queen?"

"I hope so," Metis said heavily.

If their captain was going to go around hiding mysterious women in his cabin, better a kidnapped queen than a vengeful ex-girlfriend who was apparently also a genuine mermaid.

The *Caliban* had been at sea for hours, sailing for a destination known only to the captain (and the first mate, after a very heated whisper argument between Bones and Sal), when the singing began.

Rain pattered lightly over the heads and shoulders of the crew on deck. There was just enough sun peeking through the clouds to create an eerie haze overhead, and a pair of fluttering pale rainbows for good measure.

Metis heard a few notes at first, barely audible on the northerly breeze. She thought it must be Lillit up in the crow's nest, practicing her arias for the ship's forthcoming talent contest.

But then Hobsbawn's hands went slack on the sail rope, Sal let the wind catch a map from their fingers, tearing it away across the waves, and Ginger lost interest halfway through resolving a fist-fight between two cabin sprats.

Everyone's eyes were on the water.

Metis had read a great deal of poetry in her youth, grasping at any possible source of epic adventure. Now, when she felt the music in her bones, she knew what this was. "Captain!" she cried, hands already clapped over her ears. "Sirens!"

Captain Bones laughed, his hands still steady on the wheel, his dark eyes fixed on the ocean ahead. "Not in these waters, Bosun. Don't let your imagination run away with you."

Beneath them, the water was choppy. The *Caliban* listed to one side as the rain drummed harder on to the deck. Rivulets of water poured off the sails, forming puddles.

The song rose, louder around them, coming from all sides. Every crew member on deck except for Metis and the captain took three steps closer to the rail.

"*Captain*," she said desperately.

Bones turned, and saw what she was seeing. His face changed instantly. "First Mate. Stand down. Quarter-mistress. To me!"

Sal and Ginger obeyed sluggishly, fighting something inside themselves.

The song crept under Metis' skin; whatever protection she had from magic could not fight it forever. She felt hot all over, craving nothing more than to strip off her layered shirts and breeches, and dive into the deep, cool water.

Her thoughts were filled with Calypso's face, those glorious green eyes staring into her soul…

Why had she never kissed her?

"Bosun," said Bones, his voice heavy in her ear. "*To me.*"

Metis snapped back to herself, and realised she was standing balanced on the gunwale, staring at the deep green depths below. "I —"

"Get her down, mates!"

Hands grabbed her, dragged her to the deck, now roiling around like a lobster in a pot. Rafferty, smelling strongly of onions as always, loomed over Metis and pressed something into her ears. It also smelled of onions, but when he drew away she realised that the siren song was gone, blanketed out by muffled silence.

The storm was harsher now, but she could not hear the

rain blattering on the deck. Metis looked around. She'd lost some time. The sky was darker. Doc Smedley the ship's surgeon stood on the quarter-deck, conferring with Captain Bones in sign language.

Sign language. There was one of the life skills Hekate Seabourne had left off the curriculum when hiring governesses for her daughter. Had to make room for those centuries-old pavanes and galliards, after all.

Metis headed for the captain, ready to accept any orders he could give by whatever means. She could interpret a few hand gestures, if she had to.

Smedley smacked the soaking wet map for emphasis, looking upset.

Captain Bones shook his head and turned away, white-knuckled on the wheel as he steered the wind-tossed ship directly into the deepest, wildest part of the storm.

Metis saw a glint of gold at the captain's neck, beneath his black silk shirt, which was buttoned higher than ever before. Was that a gold seashell on a chain? Had Calypso had got to him after all?

She ran at the captain, her boots sliding on the slippery deck, but Smedley stepped in her way. He cast a small light-rune in her general direction, which formed the illusion of a cute purple octopus.

Whatever he was trying to say, it could not be nearly as important as what she needed to tell him. Metis performed what she thought was a perfectly adequate mermaid mime.

Doc Smedley shook his head, frustrated, and pointed over her shoulder.

Something large and dark loomed up out of the ocean behind them. It had… a great many more shadowy tentacles than the miniature image.

Metis had got rather good at swearing (under her breath) since she embraced the life of a privateer. She was rather proud of how far she had advanced her vocabulary in that regard. What came out of her mouth over the course of the next minute was neither creative, nor under her breath. But no one could hear her, as the entire crew had wax stoppers in their ears.

Golden light fell over the ship. Every crew member who was not trying to out-stare the giant tentacled sea monster at the stern tipped their heads up to see what fresh hell had been brought down upon them.

A golden loop of light encircled the sky. It was the most impossibly large portal that Metis had ever set eyes on.

Doc Smedley raised his hands, attempting to cast some kind of charm. Metis poured what magic she had in his general direction, to feed into his spell.

Too little, too late.

The wild, choppy waters lifted the *Caliban* up, and over. Metis felt the entire ship tipping, the centre of gravity listing too far to starboard. It wasn't the giant portal or the sea monster or the sirens that was going to get them.

As always, the greatest danger was the sea itself, swallowing them whole.

IV: WE CANNOT TURN BACK

"This is not an ordinary storm," said Captain Bell. She held on to the wheel with the grim determination of a hunting hound who has finally sunk his teeth into his master's favourite slipper.

The ship's surgeon of the *Rosalind*, a tiny magister named Doncaster, lifted a charm shield up to cover half of the ship, protecting the captain and other essential personnel on the quarter-deck from the worst of the driving rain. Despite her best efforts, great swathes of water smashed down upon the stern.

No one was entirely dry, spells notwithstanding.

Thornbury had urged Mneme to stay below in relative safety. She refused, not only because she had an excellent oilskin to protect her (so many covert water repelling charms sewn into the lining!) but because being below deck during the storm caused her stomach to sway and churn in a most unladylike manner.

Thornbury swayed on his feet now, having thrown all of his spellcracking might into trying to discover why the sky was trying to kill them. Mneme hovered as close to him as she dared without interrupting, ready to catch him should he swoon to the deck from sheer exhaustion.

She had noticed that Dominic was likewise choosing to stand quite near Thornbury on the other side, while apparently not paying any attention to him at all. Mneme was not fooled. Their ghostly compatriot was braced to do a bit of spellcracker-catching, should it prove necessary. That, if nothing else, pushed him from the category of Suspicious Character into Useful Ally.

Lord Manticore towered over them all, clearly under the impression that he was the person most invested in rescuing the Queen. "We cannot turn back! Her Majesty cannot be abandoned to her fate."

"The time for turning back was three hours ago," growled Captain Bell. "Keeping my ship in one piece until we reach a safe shore is all we can hope for now!"

"The storm," said Thornbury, lowering his trembling hands. Mneme offered him a shoulder to lean upon, and he accepted it gratefully. "It has an anger to it. I could feel a magical intelligence there."

"Ay, it's always bad news when the weather shows personality," said Captain Bell, taking this information in stoic stride. "Did the flinger of storms have any message to pass on to us?"

Thornbury shook his head, pressing fingers to his temple. "Only that we are unwelcome in this part of the ocean."

"That much is obvious," said the captain. "Nice to know where we stand, even if it's up shit creek. And onward we go!"

The masts creaked above them as the *Rosalind* rushed forth into the storm.

"Is the ship safe?" Mneme asked, shouting to be heard above the wind and rain.

"That depends," replied Captain Bell. "We're following a fairy story. Does anyone remember whether, in all those pretty nursery pictures of the Isle of Dream, the island happened to be surrounded by bloody enormous, jagged rocks?"

There was a tearing sound above them. Everyone looked up, afraid the mast was about to topple… but the source of the terrible noise was something else altogether.

Mneme gazed in horror at the shape in the sky: a perfect oval, gleaming at the edges like a gilt mirror, and huge enough to swallow the ship whole. Rain fell into it from above and vanished. "That's a *portal*," she said. Her hand dipped once more into one of the pockets in her oilskin, checking that Basil the glass hedgehog was safe and well. Poor dear. He really would never want to leave home again after this adventure.

"It *can't* be," said Thornbury. "What's holding it up? Portals don't work that way."

Mneme had noticed at times that her husband's advanced magical education sometimes compromised his ability to accept new ideas. Luckily, he had a wife who had been home schooled in an extended family where wild and surprising magical experiments were par for the course.

"Oh," said Captain Bell in an oddly calm voice. "So, you're not familiar with all the tales they tell about the Isle of Dream, young man? Might be in for some surprises, then."

This time, the screeching, tearing sound was the mast, finally cracking in half. The surgeon's shield charm fell with it, letting in all the rain and more.

Water swamped the deck of the *Rosalind*, and the world.

PART II

THE ISLE OF DREAM

5

SIR FLORIMEL AND SIR FLORIZEL

Metis awoke slowly. At first, she could not open her eyes, and panicked, but she soon realised this was because her face was encrusted with damp, gritty sand.

The sun was shining. The sea was lapping gently against the shore. She was on a beach.

There was no ship.

She looked around wildly. The shore was unfamiliar, and there were no other islands in sight. No ships. No footprints on the sand. She was completely alone.

The sensible thing would be to hike inland, find a source of fresh water. But Metis was not feeling especially sensible right now. She wanted her ship and her crew. On unsteady feet, she began to make her way around the beach, calling out occasionally to catch the attention of anyone within earshot.

"Ahoy the *Caliban*!" she tried at one point, as she climbed over rocks and fallen eucalyptus trees to reach another bay.

"Ahoy," she heard back, faint and echoing but real.

Metis stumbled on the rocks once, and ran the rest of the way across the sand. Thank goodness she had not lost her boots in the… (she refused to think the word shipwreck).

As she rounded another bend in the shore, however, the sight before could not be described as anything but…

Shipwreck.

The *Caliban* had beached herself, toppled over sideways on golden sand, her hull exposed like the frilly knickers of a cabaret dancer in one of the more scurrilous drinking establishments on the Continental coast.

Metis caught her breath, looking over the curves of the ship, preparing herself to see the worst kind of damage. A broken hull, a smashed mast, the drowned bodies of her friends sticking out of the port holes… To her astonishment, the fallen *Caliban* was largely undamaged.

Perhaps it was worse on the other side.

"Ahoy?" she tried again, her voice wobbling.

"Bosun!" called a familiar voice, warm and deep and glad to see her. Captain Bones.

Metis had not realised how tightly she had dreaded losing him until now, the terror washing over her with the simultaneous rush of relief that he was alive and in one piece. Bones popped up out of a deck hatch, listing on the tilted deck. He was soaking wet, his black leathers and silks clinging tightly to his long limbs. His long, dark braids were wild and salt-crusted.

Alive.

"How is she in one piece?" Metis yelled up at him. *How are you in one piece?*

Bones bounded off the ship with frightening enthusiasm, and hurled himself in her direction. "You!" he exclaimed, half accusation and half joyful shout.

"Me?" That couldn't be right.

"Did you think I didn't know about all that covert knot tying, all those little charms you sank into my hull?"

"I mean…" Metis blinked. "That was nothing. I needed to run off some magic here and there." It had never occurred to her that anyone would notice; of course, Bones was never as oblivious as he pretended to be.

"This hull should have crunched like a dry piece of toast when it hit the beach." He stared wildly at her as if she was a cream cake. "You saved my ship, Blythe."

For one split second, she wished that he knew her real name. Still, it was hard to imagine she would feel any warmer inside if he had called her Seabourne.

Bones caught her up in a hug, scooping her off her feet, and Metis was so dizzy and delighted that she didn't care what he called her.

"Where is everyone else?" she asked his neck, the part of him nearest to her face.

"I don't know." The captain lowered her to the ground and she saw that gleam of gold again, under his loose shirt collar. He shifted away before she could get a good look at it. "Let's find our people."

Metis had not spent more than four hours at a time on dry land since she first went to sea. The majority of her recent land hours had been spent on docks, in taverns, and most recently on a tiny island covered in rocks.

She remembered dry land in a general sense, from her life before the sea. Grass, trees, flowers, houses, bramble hedges, village sweet shops, city streets full of carriages, that sort of thing.

This was not that. There was grass, trees and flowers, but nothing was familiar about any of them. The colours were all too bright, the sizes on the wrong scale: knee-high oak forests with lavender leaves… buttercups the colour of peonies… birch trees so tall you couldn't see the top of them… at one point, a foxglove with bell-like blooms large enough to hide a rowboat inside.

There was not a cloud in the sky, which suggested the storm had blown itself out. Despite the lack of rain, there were never less than three rainbows in the sky at any one time.

Magic was everywhere: in the dust and air, in the dirt and grass. Metis had been raised on and around islands that were thick with magic, but this was another level. The air was bright and heavy, and yet there was a discordant note there too, as if *even more* magic was lurking at the periphery, sinister and shadowy and somehow familiar.

Odd.

Every time Metis tried to ask Bones about Calypso, or the golden seashell he might or might not be wearing around his neck, her throat dried up and the words could not come out.

She was a Seabourne woman, daughter of powerful magisters. She knew a spell when it smacked her in the throat.

"That woman in your cabin," she managed to say at one point.

Bones gave her an impatient look. "She's not still there. I checked."

"I think you ought to tell me."

The fact that she could speak of *this* confirmed the woman under the hood had not been Calypso.

"I took an oath not to reveal her identity to anyone," Bones grumbled. "Including my crew."

Metis nodded grimly. "Bets were taken. Queen Aud was the favourite."

Bones sighed, and looked her directly in the eye. "Well, then. You don't need to ask me further questions. Needless to say, finding our guest is a matter of urgency."

Yes, Metis could see that it would be quite a problem to have wrecked their ship on a strange island and lost a queen into the bargain. "They can't have got far. The crew or anyone else."

"You'd think."

Neither of them said much for a while after that.

"Can you hear that?" asked Bones after several minutes of walking in silence. He lurched off into the jade-green shrubbery. Honestly, he was in the strangest mood today, shifting between deep gloom and a manic energy.

Metis chased after him, unable to break the habit that a year on the *Caliban* had installed in her. *Don't lose your captain.*

She smacked into his back on the other side of the shrubbery and peered around his tall frame.

For a minute, she could not quite wrap her head around what she was seeing: two men, completely covered in flower and ribbons. The effect was like a moderately sized florist shop had exploded at the same time that two knights from the Age of Chivalry were being tarred and feathered.

Both knights, if they were knights, were armed with very long javelins featuring sharpened novelty items: on one, a shark with a knife-point nose; on the other, the prow of a galleon, elongated enough to kebab half a lamb.

"Stay out of their way," muttered the captain.

"Good call," agreed Metis. "Don't get stabbed."

"Yes," said Bones levelly. "Also, one of those men is the kingdom's most dangerous necromancer."

"Wait," said Metis. "What?" She sidled around to get a better look.

"Avast, Sir Florimel!" declared one of the knights. He was decorated in violets and foxgloves, plus half a dozen other purple flowers that Metis did not recognise. "Take back the insult you laid at my lady's feet."

"Beware, Sir Florizel!" the other knight retorted. He was garbed in buttercups and dandelions, with the occasional bright white daisy to balance out all the yellow. "I shall not step back until you recant the scurrilous words you spoke about *my* lady!"

That was when things got very peculiar indeed, because Metis recognised the buttercup knight as her cousin's husband. She had not attended the recent wedding of Mneme Seabourne and Mr Thornbury, but she had met the spellcracker more than a year ago, at Cousin Henry's calamitous house party. "Mr Thornbury. What are *you* doing here?"

The two flower knights glanced at her briefly, dismissing her as a passing irritation. They returned their attention to each other, circling with their genuine if nonsensical weapons ready to strike.

Metis recognised the face of the second knight in that moment, and would have let out a cry of alarm, but Bones moved swiftly, his large hand covering her mouth.

Metis sputtered in indignation as he dragged her away from the bizarre display of chivalric posturing.

"Take your hands off me!" she protested, struggling.

"Only if you calm down, Bosun."

"Don't tell me to calm down!" she raged at him. "That man kidnapped the Duchess of Storm."

They pushed their way through two hedgerows of

different heights before Bones released her. "You never did explain how you came to be acquainted with the Duke and his family," he observed.

"That's hardly pertinent." She could kick herself for speaking so primly. Phrases like 'hardly pertinent' belonged to her old life of governesses and aunts and the marriage market. "It doesn't matter," she added in a growl.

Metis had felt so grateful, back on Ghost Island, that Bones asked no questions when they were rescuing Juno. She might have known he was saving them for later.

"Seabourne," he said now.

Metis snapped to attention, shaking off the cold chill that he had guessed somehow, her true identity. "*What?*"

"That other flower knight," he repeated. "Thornbury Seabourne. How do you know him?"

Oh. Not Mr Thornbury any more. The spellcracker took their family name when he married Mneme. There had been letters about the engagement, and several invitations to the wedding. Metis hadn't bothered to open them all, let alone reply. Her old life felt so far away.

"We're sort of related," she said vaguely. "What about you and that necromancer?" She had felt the man's magic, dark and strange, when he seized the Duchess. The kingdom's most dangerous necromancer? He wasn't so scary when covered in purple flowers.

Now it was her captain's turn to look shifty. "We're sort of related," he admitted.

That was the Teacup Isles for you.

"What's wrong with them?" Metis demanded. "That can't be normal behaviour for either of them, with all the flowers and the —" she mimed a jabbing sort of motion.

"Oh, hell," said Bones, remembering that the two knights had been on the point of, well. Stabbing each other.

He whirled back through the shrubbery, and Metis followed.

The flower knights were long gone, with only a few scattered daisies and foxgloves on the ground. No blood, at least.

"There's something very wrong with this island," said Captain Bones.

Understatement of the year.

6

THE OPPOSITE OF A TEA PARTY

Metis and Captain Bones travelled through glades of tiny trees and clambered around boulders the size of ships. They washed sand from their skin at a massive waterfall like something out of an epic poem. They ate berries, after Metis used some minor charmwork to figure out which were poisonous, and which merely suspiciously bright.

It might have been a pleasant day out, if not for the constant worry that their crew were lost at sea, and the Queen of the Teacup Isles with them.

At one point, Metis opened her mouth to ask Bones about the golden seashell around his throat, and almost got the words out… but he turned and looked at her with such a thoughtful, heated gaze that she let out nothing but a small, rather embarrassing gasp.

When she was washing her hands and face in the deep basin at the foot of the waterfall, she thought for a moment that she saw a pair of deep emerald eyes in the water, but forgot them the second that she looked away.

After the waterfall, Bones and Metis came across a

twinkling, crystalline plaza laid out on a brilliant green expanse of lawn beside the steep bank of a river. The hills around them were matted with wild, scrubby plants, but this lawn was like something from a country estate, perfectly manicured.

At least, it had been perfectly manicured before some kind of tea party massacre took place, leaving smashed teacups and upturned food plates scattered all over the shining crystal plaza, smeared here and there with whipped cream and jam.

(Perhaps a wedding, not a tea party. Metis was reminded of the last-but-one wedding she had attended, the one that ruined her mamma's reputation in the eyes of society — that also featured a flurry of teacups and food hurled all about a bright green lawn.)

"Oh, no!" exclaimed someone. It was a jolt for Metis to hear another human voice. (Not human, as it turned out.)

"Oh, no, oh no, oh, no!" A bedraggled green figure came up the riverbank, head sagging in despair. He was an extraordinary sight: exactly like a butler in a tailored grey morning coat… except that the suit was soaking wet, and the butler was a frog. "Just look at this mess!" groaned the frog butler.

"Excuse me," called Metis, finding the manners of her old life before the *Caliban* rising to the fore. "Can you tell us what happened here, good sir?"

Bones silently mouthed the words 'good sir' as if he had been raised in a barn.

The frog turned dramatically to face them. "The Queen's hunt, I suppose," he said tragically. "That's what usually happens around here. Such a mess, what a calamity! And I had the tea things arranged so nicely for Miss Calypso's guests."

Captain Bones went very still.

"You know Calypso?" Metis exclaimed, a little surprised she was able to let the name emerge from her mouth.

"Oh, yes," said the frog butler, puffing up with satisfaction. "I've served Miss Calypso's family all my life."

"Her family. Captain, did you hear that?" Calypso's family lived here, on this island? Did that mean more mermaids, or was she only one?

Captain Bones glowered at Metis. "Where did the Queen's hunt go?" he demanded of the butler. "What Queen are you talking about?"

"I don't know where they go," said the droopy green creature, fluttering his webbed hands in a melodramatic fashion. "They ride here, they ride there. In and out of the river. I thought this would be far enough away to be safe." He looked sadly at the chaotic mess of crockery and cakes. "Miss Calypso will be so very disappointed."

"She's coming here," said Metis. "You expect her soon?"

Calypso could explain this strange place. Perhaps she was the reason they were here at all — her and her golden seashells.

"Come on," Captain Bones said roughly. He set out towards the riverbank, not looking back to see if Metis was following. "We'll head downriver. If her Majesty is here, we have to find her."

"Never mind the Queen," Metis yelled after his retreating back. "Don't you want to see Calypso?" She could barely get the last few words out, as her throat tightened, making her cough wildly.

"I'd offer you tea," said the frog butler in gloomy tones, producing a broom from behind a nearby tree and beginning the work of tidying up the meadow. "But we're fresh out of cups."

Bones had not gone far. Metis caught up to him at the edge of the river, still coughing. "You can't just pretend it's not —" she said, but couldn't manage any more. Clearly the charm was still active, preventing Calypso from being discussed in any detail. The magical compulsion tasted like ginger and pepper on her tongue.

So much for Doc Smedley managing to destroy the thing. It was still working against her, though it only existed as a few purple lines.

Bones signalled for silence.

Metis was about to snap something unbearably rude when she realised he was staring into thin air.

"A creature bit me," he muttered.

"An insect?"

"Wouldn't that be nice."

Metis peered more closely. She could see glittering motes of something in the air, hovering just in front of Bones. Too small to focus upon, even if…

Sunlight gleamed off cobweb wings.

"Are those fairies?" she gasped.

"I hope so," said Bones. "Or there is something *very* wrong with my eyesight."

Metis leaned in, her shoulder brushing his upper arm. If you concentrated hard enough, you could see tiny bodies suspended between those fragile, fluttering wings. And…

"Ow! One stung me," she complained.

A sparkle of pink and green flew at her face even as she rubbed her cheek, and for a moment she stared her attacker full in the face. "Lillit?"

"The one that bit me looked just like Damon," growled Bones. "That one's Hobsbawn, right? What in hellfire has happened to my crew?"

"Hello, it's us," Metis said, enunciating slowly. "Do you know who we are?"

The able seaman fairies grew angrier, buzzing around their faces with intensity.

"Stand down, shipmates!" the captain commanded them.

Metis took his hand, threading her fingers into his. She could not have imagined doing such a thing yesterday, but here they were. "Captain," she said calmly. "I don't think they have the slightest idea who we are. Who *they* are."

If Lillit had transformed into a fairy, and kept her own mind, she would be dancing a jig, spinning cartwheels in the air, playing pranks from her tiny new height. As for her husbands: Damon and Hobsbawn would rather cut off each other's legs than attack their captain.

Bones' fingers pressed against hers. He allowed Metis to drag him down the river path, away from their tiny menaces. "It was the same with the others," he muttered. "Seabourne and Dom. This place has infected our crew, made them forget themselves. Transformed them into… that. And the crew of at least one other ship."

If Mr Thornbury was here, and that necromancer — Metis was not going to ignore the fact that Bones knew his first name — then the Duke and Duchess of Storm might be on the island. Mneme, too.

Queen Aud. The crew of the *Caliban*. All of them at the mercy of whoever was in charge around here — presumably, the same person who paid the salaries of frog butlers.

Miss Calypso's family. An island peopled with mermaids. "Perhaps we should stay away from large bodies of water," she considered.

"Why would you and I be immune to the curse?" Bones asked no one in particular.

That, Metis could answer, even if she was not able to use words to do it. She squeezed his hand and let go, then reached up to touch the side of his unshaven cheek. As he stared down at her in surprise, she thought very hard about kissing him.

She had a theory about the charm that stopped her talking about Calypso or the golden shell. She had circumvented it briefly because she was so surprised at the frog butler mentioning Calypso. As soon as she thought about it, her throat dried up again.

Time to not think about it. The easiest thing in the world was to think about kissing her captain. Part of her brain had been fighting that particular impulse all year.

Metis gazed up and into his eyes, imagining what it might feel like, if his arms came around her, his face tilted down a little further… and now she could see his dark eyes widening slightly as if he knew exactly was on her mind.

Bones didn't seem to hate the idea. In fact, as she held him with her gaze, he leaned down just slightly, and…

Her other hand moved fast, catching hold of the chain at his throat.

Startled, Bones blinked at her.

Metis tugged hard on the golden seashell, and gave him a pointed look.

"Oh," said Bones, and she could see the thought dawning on him. "But…"

Metis thought about kissing him again, and moved her other hand from his face, keeping it open, so he could see the purple lines of the seashell mark emblazoned on her palm.

His expression changed. "Where did you get that?" Bones barked, all worry and fury.

Metis was all tangled up now in what she could or could not say, what she should or should not think. She thought about Calypso in the water, the flick of that dratted mermaid tail. But Bones was not telepathic, and merely thinking the answer wasn't going to be helpful.

"Same as you," she managed to say, before her lips clamped shut and she was overtaken by the worst coughing fit of her life.

At least that should keep them both from any kissing thoughts for a while. Hardly attractive, to be hacking up her lungs on the grass.

Finally, Metis felt her breathing calm down. She gave Bones a reassuring if watery grin and a thumbs up.

He dropped to the ground on the grassy bank, tipping his face up to the sky with a tragic air. "This is all my fault."

Was Metis going to have to be stern with him? She didn't think she had it in her, not after the day she'd had. She collapsed next to him on the grass. "That is a drastic misreading of events, Captain," she said, poking him in the ribs.

"I should never have trusted her," he muttered. "I knew she had secrets. I let her in anyway. Shared everything. And now I've lost my ship, my crew, the *Queen*…"

"No," Metis said sharply. She prodded him again, more sharply this time. "You've lost nothing. Your crew, the ship. Everything you love is right here on this island." Including Calypso, most likely. "We're a little scattered and confused right now," she added. "And apparently there are frog butlers. But it could be worse."

Bones let out a guttural groan, and tipped himself to one side, so he was looking directly at her. "You're right," he sighed. "All we have to do is locate a missing queen, crack the spell holding our mates in thrall, probably fight the island in some kind of dramatic magical showdown, and get our ship back in the water."

"Exactly," said Metis, well aware of how ridiculous they both sounded right now. "That's like, an afternoon's work. Tops."

The captain laughed, still looking a bit wild, but a whole lot less lost. "I never knew you were such a bright-eyed optimist, Bosun Blythe."

She kicked him lightly with her foot. "Someone has to be, with a sad sack like you in charge, Cap'n Bones."

7

RIGHT THIS WAY, YOUR TABLE'S WAITING

When Metis was seven or so, her father caught her trimming a bonnet with tiny, intricate ribbon spells.

Her mamma insisted that Metis focus upon the proper magics for a lady, and so there was always another bonnet to trim. Adding your own embroidered flowers or ribbons or bows was the best way to stand out, Mamma insisted. Just like dancing and croquet and any other ornamental skills a lady might learn, the ultimate goal was to demonstrate one's magical accomplishments to a potential husband.

"What are you doing?" Gaulliver Seabourne barked when he saw his little daughter on her knees, pressing ribbon violets into the band of a bonnet that was far too large for her.

"Making it pretty," said Metis, always startled when he spoke to her.

"What's the point in that?" To her shock, he knelt down beside her, and added his own forceful row of ribbon violets to the trim, each of them sizzling with a contained but powerful flare of magic. "Good fortune, luck at cards, protection against poisons, warding against ill-intent, shield from other magic users," he said, tapping each violet in turn. "Just because something is pretty, child, does not mean it should have no function."

Metis frowned up at him. "It also protects my face from the sun."

Her father laughed, a rare occurrence in this unhappy household. "Wouldn't want to make those freckles worse, I suppose."

That particular bonnet had lasted longer than any other; no matter how many times it got squashed or dropped or lost over the years, it was always to be found, pristine and tidy, in the hall cupboard.

She might hate her father for disappearing as he had (not to mention, for disparaging her excellent freckles!) but she took his lesson to heart. Whenever Metis added an embroidered flower or ribbon trim to any gown or hand-kerchief or pocket, she would sneak in a tiny spell. Some-thing useful.

She didn't even need a needle and thread.

That was, perhaps, how she had got the idea to let her spare magic out into the hull of the *Caliban*, adding small protections here and there whenever she laid her hand against the curved planks or scratched a nail against the decking. Bonnets to trim were few and far between onboard, though Bosun Blythe had offered up her embroi-dery skills a few times when someone had a petticoat to mend, or a hem that needed prettying.

Now Metis was stuck on an island full of strange magics, hiking over hills and dales in the company of a captain under the thrall of a seashell. They needed all the protection they could get.

Bones with his long legs was always slightly ahead of

her. Whenever Metis caught up, she would add an extra tiny embroidered flower to the back of his shirt, where he couldn't see it. Black violets seemed appropriate, and discreet enough against his black silk. She imbued each violet with a small protection: against ill-intent, or foreign magic, or poisons. It might be too little, too late, but Metis was tired of feeling hopeless. She could do this.

She added a few marigold petals to her cuffs too, imbuing the petals with further protections. After seeing what the island had done to Lillit and her husbands, they had to be ready for anything. *Protection against transformation, protection against losing your mind…*

They did not stop to rest, and the small magics she was performing took more out of Metis than she had expected. She was about ready to drop: hungry, thirsty and so homesick for the *Caliban* that she thought she might die of it.

When Bones crested a hill covered in bright red poppies, Metis briefly considered sliding down into the wildflowers for a nap. Perhaps he would not notice.

(He glanced back five seconds later; she wouldn't have had time to close her eyes.) "There's a ship," he informed her.

That jolted Metis alert. "What do you mean, a ship?" She stumbled forward to join him.

On the far side of the hill was a wide chequerboard meadow, every square a different shade of green. The long grasses shimmered back and forth, like the tide coming in on the shore. And in the centre… a ship.

"Not our ship," she said immediately. The wood was too dark, and the prow too chunky. The port holes were the wrong size. Also, they knew where their ship was: the *Caliban* was beached on the far side of the island.

"I know her," Bones said in a low voice. "I've seen her before."

"Is that a tree growing out of her deck?"

Where there should be a mast, there was a rough trunk with wide branches, dripping with apple blossom though it was completely the wrong time of year.

"Come on," Bones said, and grabbed Metis' hand like that was a normal thing they did, the two of them. He kept his pace to hers for once, approaching the new ship with caution.

There was a figurehead on front: a carved woman with her bosom partially uncovered (usual) and her head missing (quite *unusual*). Where there had once been a nameplate attached to the hull, there was a cracked hole that someone had stuffed with freshly picked roses.

Bones hesitated, then knocked his knuckles against the hull. "I know her. The *Rosalind*."

"How is she staying upright?" Metis might not be an expert on sailing ships, but she knew that to find one balancing on her keel in a meadow was about as normal as a frog in a tailcoat.

Like everywhere else on this island, the air smelled of salt and flowers and magic.

Captain and bosun stared up at the *Rosalind*. A gleaming rope ladder billowed out from over the wale, slapping the side of the hull.

Metis' eye was caught by a thread-like pattern on the hull itself, jagged shapes suggesting the curved planks had been smashed and carefully fitted back together. "Do you think —" she started to say, but Bones was already climbing.

She wasn't *not* going to follow him.

The deck was clean. A working ship was never entirely pristine no matter how hard you scrubbed and swabbed, but the *Rosalind* gleamed as if newly built. As if she had never been allowed anywhere near an ocean. There wasn't a speck of salt in her creases, nor a spot of sun-bleach on her sail.

It was creepy.

Metis could feel the presence of bodies beneath her — music floating through the hatch, and a vibration of talking, or singing, or complaining. Somewhere in the depths of this ship, there was a crew.

"There you are!" said a voice behind them.

Metis jumped, and was relieved to see she wasn't the only one; Bones almost fell over in his startlement.

Here was Sal, wearing a long white (too bright) sheepskin coat over a smart navy-striped shirt and breeches. Their first mate strode past them both, tossing a watch back and forth on a chain.

"Where did you get that?" Bones asked, as if he'd seen a ghost.

"You're late," said Sal with a stern look, so familiar that Metis thought she might cry. "Come this way, your table's waiting."

"Our table," Bones repeated. "Wait, let me take a look at that watch."

The gold chain slithered safely inside Sal's pocket. Sal flung open the hatch as if it didn't usually take at least two crew members to do that on their own ship. The music was louder, now — fiddle strings twanging behind and a slow, crooning voice.

Sal leaped down into the depths of the ship.

"Something's wrong with them," said Metis.

"That's my brother's watch," growled Bones, and took Metis' hand again to drag her through the hatch.

They were holding hands as they made their way down the rickety steps together into what should be a cargo hold… but was instead a tavern, lit with a hissing oil lamp at every table.

Metis blinked, her eyes adjusting.

There was Ginger, singing a smoochy torch song from a small stage built from barrels. She wore a killer red dress that looked like it had been nicked from backstage at the Ophelian Pleasure Gardens. Rabbit ears stuck out from her long, titian hair.

Doc Smedley and Gunner Fry sat at a nearby table, holding hands over a dish of spiced mussels.

"That's Captain Bell," said Bones in a hoarse voice, indicating an elderly woman with bare, muscled arms pouring ales at the bar. Her tattoos featured four skulls, six swords and fourteen different full-coloured flowers, and that was just one arm. "She must have brought the *Rosalind* here. That's how our flower knights made it to the island."

Metis gave him a stern look. "You never did explain exactly how you knew that necromancer."

"No," said Bones. "Want to chat about how you're related to that spellcracker?"

Sal saved them both by appearing before them, whisking a cleaning cloth over the table. "Main course is oysters or walrus," they announced. "Done three ways, and it's best you ask no further details."

"Sal," urged Metis. "Do you recognise us?"

Sal's face, grumpy by default, stretched into a sort of artificial rictus. "You're our honoured guests. Lobster pate is off — they ran away, don't blame 'em. Vegetarian option is kelp gelatine, but I wouldn't recommend that to anyone I liked."

"Whatever you recommend," said Bones, his eyes fixed on his first mate. "We trust you, Sal."

"Please not the walrus," Metis added in a small voice. Sal had already turned to and hurtled back through the galley door.

Bones brushed a hand again Metis' shoulder as if he

really was escorting her to some fine dining experience. "I'll see what I can find out at the bar."

"Mine's a cider," said Metis, taking her seat.

He quirked a small smile at her that warmed her to her toes, damn it, and went off to ask awkward questions of the captain of the *Rosalind* — who, quite likely, knew as little about what was going on here as they did.

"Mermaids can never be trusted," crooned Ginger. "Every affair is kiss and shell..."

Metis gave her a hard stare, but the quartermistress continued to sing blank-faced, as if she knew no one in the audience.

"Truth fish," announced Sal, returning to the table with two tiny plates of brilliant teal ceramic. They slapped down both plates in front of Metis, along with real linen napkins featuring embroideries of various kinds of octopus.

"Excuse me?"

"It's an amooz-boosh. That means tiny, unsatisfying food that moves the story forward."

The fish were indeed tiny — glazed peach-coloured sardines the size of anchovies, laid out on pieces of dry toast the size of a coin. They sparkled with a scatter of salmon roe, and actually did look delicious.

Metis was reminded of the adventures of Bonny Blythe, her favourite storybook when she was a child. "If I eat this," she murmured. "Do I double in size?"

"If you eat it," said Sal. "You'll find the answers you'll seeking."

Metis lifted her eyes from the plate to meet the steady gaze of the first mate, one of the people she trusted most in the world. "Sal," she breathed. "What's happening here?"

"Find him at the summer palace," warbled the

songstress on the stage. "Swim along, don't lose your head…"

That wasn't Ginger.

Metis straightened up. Sal was already off to the kitchen of mystery again, presumably to find the right platter for serving walrus. In her peripheral vision, Metis could see Bones turning around at the bar stool to see…

Calypso was singing on the tavern stage. She wore a dress like something you might see at the opera — full dress, Mamma would have called it, the short-sleeved gown cinched in tight at the bodice and overrun with patterns of lace and pearl beading in contrast to the brilliant green of the silk.

Calypso's feet were bare. No tail. So, not a mermaid? Sometimes a mermaid? Metis only had the slightest idea how it might work. In stories, mermaids could shift sometimes from human form to…

Calypso had feet on the *Caliban*, she reminded herself sternly, so as not to get too distracted. The scales came later.

Bones looked wrecked. He lurched up from the bar stool, arrowing directly for the stage. Calypso met his eyes for a moment, and her lips formed a small, sad smile.

Then she filled her lungs and screamed.

"The Queen's hunt is coming! Run for your lives!"

Everyone in the tavern reacted as if they knew exactly what those words meant. They tumbled this way and that, making for one side of the hold, which cracked like an egg. Shards of planking fell away, revealing the grassy meadow, and a tidal wave of water rushing towards them.

"Jump!" Doc Smedley shouted at Metis before he leaped out of the hold, hand in hand with Gunner Fry.

Metis was shoved from behind, ending up near the massive hole in the side of the ship.

The approaching water wasn't so much a tidal wave as a channel of seawater, zig-zagging its way like a floating sea-serpent across the grass. Large enough to swallow them all whole.

Metis jumped, landing on the soft grass.

Everyone from the *Rosalind* who made it out of the ship in time ran in different directions, strewing hats and cups and napkins as they fled. Metis saw the channel of water lash out sideways, knocking two able seamen off their feet. Then it whirled back in the direction of the *Rosalind*.

There were creatures inside the water. A pageant of riders on horseback, but some of the horses weren't exactly horses. The one in front had sharpened teeth and scales instead of a glossy coat. Its rider wore a streaming teal silk cape, and had no head upon her neck — her head, covered in long grey braids like a classic sea witch, was mounted on a staff which she raised in triumph.

The next creature had wild, curling horns and clawed feet. Another had spiky wings, and yet another looked like a jellyfish with hooves. The wild pageant of horses and monsters and ocean smashed into the *Rosalind*, scattering the pieces of the ship up into the air in a burst of saltwater.

Had this happened before? Metis remembered those cracks in the hull… and then she realised she hadn't seen Captain Bones since she jumped free of the ship.

Before she could shout his name, the wild water pageant turned back in her direction. It was too late to run, not that Metis had the speed or skill to outrun a magical monster stampede.

The steed in front of the stampede now was a manticore. Huge, larger than any horse, with the head of a man, the mane of a lion, the body of… whatever a manticore had for a body, possibly more lion… the lashing stinging tail of a scorpion. All blue and purple and strange as if it was a sea monster and not a clearly land-based mythical creature like in all the story books.

This manticore rider (who did have a head) laughed merrily without losing her towering silver crown. Metis knew her face. It appeared on every coin in the Teacup Isles.

Queen Aud.

The ocean pageant collided with Metis with a roar and a scream. She fell to the ground, trampled by creatures and hooves and water, so much water, filling the world, filling her lungs…

Drowning in a meadow was not a future she had imagined for herself, when she ran away to sea.

8

WHAT ANGEL WAKES ME FROM MY FLOWERY BED?

*D*rowning was warm. Metis felt comfortable, wrapped in the arms of someone she trusted beyond all things. There weren't many people who could make her feel that way.

She opened her eyes, and saw Calypso.

Mermaid.

Metis was lying on a carpet of flowers in a grotto that must have once been part of a house — or a palace. It had all manner of curled, gilded furniture, all swallowed up by thick vines and bold, brightly coloured flowers.

There was antique wallpaper running up the walls to an impossibly high ceiling, with slitted windows throwing muted light down upon them.

Below her, there was a pool. It looked natural, with rocky edges rather than tiles, but the colours were a brilliant teal and violet, which were not the least bit natural.

Calypso lounged, her tail half-submerged in the waters of the low pool. Metis could see the pattern of her green scale from her hips and belly all the way down to where the shape was quite clearly tail, not legs. Calypso wore a loose white muslin shirt over a dark singlet that showed through the light fabric — the kind of easy outfit she might have thrown on when it was time to scrape whelks off the hull on a hot day, and yet the effect was almost worse than if she was baring her breasts like the saucy mermaids on illustrated maps.

Her golden hair was that in-between fuzzy stage between being wet and dry, which stung Metis with nostalgia for when they were friends. For a brief moment, before she realised Metis was awake, Calypso looked heavy and exhausted.

Metis caught a breath, and Calypso's brilliant green eyes snapped to her. She smiled.

Unfair.

"Is this the Summer Palace?" Metis asked.

Calypso's tail twitched in the water. "It's the Tropical Palace."

"How many palaces does one island need?"

"You'd be surprised!" Calypso gave a dry sort of laugh. "The Isle of Dream has a thing about queens. When it worries they might not be happy here, it starts sprouting palaces like tomato plants. This one's been empty for decades. Queen Ianthe thought that Aud and Orion might settle here after the wedding." She bit her lip, darting a glance at Metis.

Who's Orion? What wedding?

"Aud," Metis repeated. "Queen of the Teacup Isles."

Calypso stared back defiantly. "She'll be Queen of the Isle of Dream soon enough."

"Instead of, or as well as?"

There was a long pause. Metis felt the silence fill up with unspoken questions. One loomed rather large above the others. *Why did you leave us?*

"What's going on?" she asked instead. "Seriously. What on earth have you dragged us into?"

"I'm sorry," said Calypso, which wasn't a proper answer. "I really am, Bonny. I wanted to keep you all well out of it, but the *Caliban*… it had to be the *Caliban* who brought her here. She was the only ship I knew well enough, the only crew I trusted…"

"The *Caliban* was lucky to make it to these shores in one piece," Metis fumed.

Calypso blinked at that, looking surprised. "She wasn't wrecked?"

Oh, there was the anger Metis has been suppressing, bubbling away under her ribs. "You didn't check?"

"I've been busy! I've been trying to fix things, and my mother is being impossible, and the island's magic keeps spiralling out of control, so every time I get close, all my work is undone…"

That, at least, was something Metis could understand. "What needs fixing?" she asked.

Calypso laughed. "Oh, I knew you were a born bosun. I felt it in my gills."

For a moment, just for a moment, it felt like they were on the same side.

"Most of my job these days is picking up the pieces," Metis muttered.

"I know how that feels, too." Calypso held her gaze. "How's Sal doing in my old job?"

Metis did not ask how Calypso knew about that. "They haven't broken anyone's hearts lately, so better than average."

Calypso nodded, glancing away as the sting hit. "Got it."

"But also," Metis went on, her voice rising. "I don't

know where Sal is right now. Last I saw them, they didn't recognise me. Same goes for Ginger, and Lillit. All of them. Our crew are scattered across this island without their memories. Some of them don't even have the right bodies. Why would you do that to us, just to steal a queen?"

"I told you," Calypso said softly. "I'm trying to fix things."

Metis was trying to understand. "What needs to be fixed?"

"This island. My family."

"*We* were your family." Metis couldn't stand any more of this. She stood up in a hurry, feeling dizzy. The strange, bright flowers under her feet pressed against her ankles, as if they didn't want her to leave. "Fix us," she snarled. "Fix the crew. You did this to us."

"I know. I'm sorry."

"Stop saying that!"

Calypso's tail twitched miserably, rising and flopping in the water as if she had no control of it.

Metis could not help but stare. "Were you always a mermaid?"

"In a manner of speaking."

"Why don't you have a straight answer for anything?"

The tail splashed twice, and then two pink feet stuck out of the bubbles for a moment. Calypso reached for a bright-coloured length of silk, and wrapped it around her hips as she rose out of the water, standing on those brand new feet. "I need you to help me, Bonny," she said.

Metis clamped her lips over her first response, which was yes. Her first instinct was always going to be yes, where Calypso was concerned. It was getting to be a problem. "You don't deserve my help."

Calypso nodded. "I can't protect our crew from the island, or my mother. Not entirely. I need you to do it."

"Your mother?"

"Queen Ianthe."

Well, that explained a lot.

"What do you need me to do?" Metis asked grudgingly.

Calypso raised her hand as if about to touch Metis' hair, and a bright blue flower with round petals spiralled on a stem around her arm, extending towards Metis. It looked like a single forget-me-not flower, only it was the size of a teapot. "This will help."

Metis stepped out of range. "You think after that business with the seashell, I'd trust you with another gift?"

"It's not a gift," Calypso urged, reaching her arm nearer. "This is *my* flower. I'm lending it to you. That's important," she added, and now her fingers were in Metis' hair. The flower unwound its stem from Calypso's arm and slid into Metis' hair like a serpent seeking a warm place to sleep. She could feel it tightening in her unkempt blue curls.

Metis breathed harder. She wouldn't cry. Not in front of Calypso, after everything. "I don't trust you," she said through gritted teeth.

"You don't have to," Calypso said immediately. "Just keep the crew together long enough to escape. With the *Caliban* in one piece you'll be able to make it, all of you. Don't let my mud dirty your boots."

Metis wanted to slap her, or scream at her, or kiss her. Behind her, she felt a rising pulse of magic that was entirely familiar. "Is that a portal?"

Before she could turn to look, Calypso pushed her through.

~

Metis landed on the deck of a ship. For one moment, she thought she was home on the *Caliban*. As she rolled to her feet and the ship stayed deadly still, she realised the truth — even before she fully recovered her sensibilities from the sudden portal travel, she knew where she was.

The *Rosalind*, rebuilt again. This poor ship.

They were not in a meadow now. The *Rosalind* was still balanced impossibly upright, though now she was tucked between two sand dunes, pointed towards a beach.

The sky was beginning to lose the light of the day, with crisp sunset colours bleeding in from the horizon. It was not the same beach where Metis had last seen the *Caliban*. It could be the other side of the island, for all she knew.

The island's magic keeps spiralling out of control. She had assumed there was a menace behind all this turmoil, with this Queen Ianthe and her hunt at the heart of it. How could they fight an island?

Not that privateers had a marvellous history of defying queens… not without becoming lawless pirates.

Down on the sand, there was the crackle of a bonfire. Strange shapes lurched up off the sand: spiralling staircases and gothic arches like a mighty palace had been constructed out of seashells and driftwood.

The beasts of the Queen's hunt lolled around on the sand, or in the shallows of the ocean: the horses and not-horses, the magical sea-creatures and more. The teal and purple manticore that Metis had last seen being ridden by Queen Aud.

Further up the beach, ladies were running and screaming together, laughing maniacally. They were barefoot and wild, and Metis knew some of them.

Queen Aud, yes — carefree and merry as Metis had never imagined she could be from the few formal glimpses she had ever been accorded during the Season. Her black curly hair was wild and unrestrained by its usual nets of pearl or jewelled tiaras.

There was Lady Hadderine Bustledown, Mistress of the Robes, a lady-in-waiting so ancient and terrifying that even Metis' mamma had been intimidated when their paths crossed in assembly halls. Tonight, Lady H wore a headdress of gilded horns, and had flowers daubed on her bare legs and arms in bright blue ink. Mamma would not approve… but neither would Lady H if she were in her right mind.

Sailors, too — mostly women, a few familiar faces from the *Caliban*, and others that Metis only knew from taverns where the crews of other ships met up from time to time. Captain Bell of the *Rosalind*, perhaps the only one on the sand who was older than Lady Hadderine, wore nothing but body paint and her own ship's flag draped around her like a gown.

Mneme. Cousin Mneme was there, dancing with Queen Aud. Her red hair streamed wildly behind her like they were children again, running around the grounds of Shellwich Standing, and no one was out in Society or had to worry about such things as marriage and matchmaking and mammas.

The queen's ladies danced, they cavorted, they *sang*. The accompanying music came from everywhere, as if the driftwood palace had a drunken orchestra trapped within every shell.

Metis had no wish to go any nearer, but she couldn't stay on the beached *Rosalind* all night. Not when her crew were out of their minds thanks to this dratted island.

She climbed down the side with the assistance of a rope ladder and set out over the dunes, almost tripping over Ginger.

The quartermistress was now dressed like a housemaid

rather than a glamorous cabaret singer (though, as this was Ginger, she still looked glamorous in apron and mob cap). She sat on the sandy grass with a giant silver tray of sausages on sticks resting beside her. Ginger looked exhausted and annoyed, her boots abandoned a few feet away.

As Metis approached, Ginger barely glanced in her direction. "I hate hen parties," she announced, as if it was a normal phrase to say aloud.

Metis did not understand the reference.

Ginger rolled her eyes, which was familiar enough to be comforting. "The night before the nuptials," she explained. "Brides go wild with their friends. Forget they're ladies, if you know what I mean. Like the maenads of old, all wine and bare flesh. Mind you," she added thoughtfully. "The gentlemen aren't much better."

"They don't do that where I come from," said Metis primly. The last wedding she had attended, between the Duke of Storm and his new Duchess, had occasioned no merriment the night before — though it was a small family affair, almost an elopement.

The wedding before that *was* an elopement, if it still counted as such when the groom had been kidnapped and enchanted into being there. (Metis was starting to suspect that *this* wedding, if it was for Queen Aud and this Orion fellow, was more of the same.)

Metis had attended her share of wedding teas, but they were mostly prim affairs, attended by as many aunts as young ladies. (And the aunts did not wear body paint and horns, *Lady Hadderine*.) If there were secret maenad parties for ladies about to be married, she had never been invited to one.

"They do on ships," said Ginger with a smirk. "Though there's none of this gender separation nonsense, and the party doesn't end when the ceremony starts. When Lillit, Damon and Hobsbawn got hitched, we didn't stop dancing for six days."

"Sounds nice," said Metis, then stared at her friend. If she remembered that wedding… "Ginger. Do you know who I am?"

"Of course I —" Ginger turned towards her, and her mouth fell open. "*Bonny.*"

"You're you again."

"I was —" Ginger scowled. "I was their serving maid. For hours."

It hadn't been hours for Metis. "And before that?"

"Singing in a tavern. I saw you. And Captain Bones…" Ginger blinked. "Before that, it was a picnic. Near a river, with us all sitting about on a crystal floor holding porcelain cups like idiots. The Queen's hunt tore through that, too…" She blinked again, her heavy lashes making her eyes look more startled than usual. "Am I going mad or was Calypso there?"

"She was," said Metis. "We came through after that picnic was wrecked by the Queen's hunt."

Every time the queens and their chaotic sea friends crashed through part of the island, it was as if everyone got jumbled in their thoughts, even their identities. From what Calypso said, the island itself was behind it all.

Ginger's thoughts seemed clear now. "We?"

"Captain Bones was with me."

The quartermistress nodded, then leaned towards Metis with a thoughtful sniff. "Your hair smells amazing."

"Thank you?" Metis wasn't entirely comfortable with where this was going. Ginger had always been an equal opportunity flirt, but it was hardly the time.

"No, I mean it. Where did you get that flower?"

Metis had almost forgotten the bright blue bloom that

Calypso set in her hair. When Ginger moved back from sniffing Metis' hair, her gaze was sharper than ever. "Lillit and Hobsbawn and Damon are all *fairies*," she exclaimed.

"Yes," agreed Metis. "Did you just remember?"

"We have to find them," Ginger said urgently. "If that flower of yours can fix whatever spell keeps tossing us about, then we can get our crew back."

More than anyone else, even including the captain, it was the quartermaster's (or mistress's) job to manage the crew. To ensure everyone was safe, well and receiving appropriate justice. That was why the position was elected in the first place.

Oh, it was such a relief to have Ginger back where she belonged: worrying about them all. Metis had felt so alone. She did not know what to think about Calypso's magical token, but she wasn't going to look a gift seahorse in the mouth.

"Should we start with Queen Aud?" she asked, thinking about the original mission, the one that the captain had never entirely confided in them.

"Screw that," said Ginger. "No queens. No one connected to that damned hunt. We don't know how long your little blue flower is going to hold out. We start with Sal, and then we find our captain."

9

DON'T LOSE YOUR HEAD

It shouldn't be this easy, to kidnap a first mate.

Even a first mate who was not remotely in their right mind.

Sal trotted back and forth on the sand alongside several frog butlers, carrying trays of wine and honey cakes and cucumber sandwiches to the dancing, lolling ladies of the court. Sal was even dressed like one of the frog butlers, with a tailcoat, bow tie and gloves (appropriate for butlering in the evenings, Metis recalled from her old life). They looked *subservient*. It was rather disconcerting.

Metis and Ginger crept around the edge of the dunes, beyond the seashell castle where the food was being delivered. Here, they found another ship, a lot like the *Rosalind*, but an older ruin. Its hull had barely survived, half of it mashed beneath the weight of the beach, and every other piece of planking was missing. It looked like the skeleton of a ship, only twice as sad.

There was not an inch of sailcloth or rope left aboard, and what remained of the deck was slanted and broken, bleached nearly white by years of unrelenting sun.

Here, where a rough hole had been carved from the hull and a makeshift counter made from a plank and two nails, was the source of all those trays full of tasty treats.

Rafferty had made himself at home. The grouchy cook of the *Caliban* was all smiles and fresh-baked bread, here in his shipwrecked beach shack. He wore a ballooning white chef's hat, and a coat decorated with black and white checks. Most disturbingly, he was cheerful as he loaded new batches of sandwiches, cakes and wine on to every tray. There was whistling.

Metis and Ginger watched from behind a scrubby, wind-whipped tree barely large enough to cover them both.

"If I grab Sal's feet and you put a hand over their mouth," Ginger considered.

"They'll kick you and bite me," Metis predicted.

"Better that than the other way around."

"*Better for who?*"

"You need to stick that flower in their face. Whatever it takes."

Metis brushed a fingertip against the giant forget-me-not still resting in their hair. "What if it only works once?"

Ginger gave her a sharp grin. "Then you wasted it on me."

"No, I didn't." Metis had no regrets. Ginger had kept an eye out for her ever since she joined the *Caliban*. She was a reassuring presence to have at her side. "We missed our chance," she noted with a groan.

Sal had loaded up with more refreshments — foaming cocktails served in upside down conch shells that balanced impossibly *en pointe* on their tray — and was already heading back across the sand towards the wild screams and wine song of the hen party.

"We'll get 'em on the next round," said Ginger with a nod.

They sat quietly together on the dunes, close enough to hear the waves crashing on the sands.

"Wait, you were *at* that wedding?" Metis said suddenly, remembering what Ginger had said as she began to remember who she was. "Lillit and Hobsbawn and Damon. Wasn't their wedding twenty years ago? You must have been a baby."

"Bless you," said Ginger, patting her on the hand. "I was fourteen. I'd only been on the *Miranda* a few months — this was before we had the *Caliban*. That party," she added, "Was when I got up the courage to tell Captain Hartigan he'd hired a cabin *girl* and not a boy."

Metis had heard plenty of tales about Captain Hartigan and the old days on the *Miranda*, but didn't know enough about the man to guess what happened next. "How did he take it?"

Ginger laughed. "He puffed himself up, tugged on his beard, and said: 'when I were a lad, it were considered unlucky to have a woman on board. Those were dull times, lass,' and then he shoved me forward to catch Lillit's bouquet."

"Sweet." Metis was relieved.

"He was a good captain," Ginger agreed. "Old fashioned, but took time to learn. Six months after the wedding, we brought Sal aboard — they were barely taller than one of the grain barrels back then, and we had to drop boy and girl from the job description altogether!"

"Oh, that's why we call them cabin sprats?" Metis had wondered.

"Could be worse. I hear on the *Ariel* they call the young'uns cabin *whelks*. I'd rather be a sprat than a whelk."

Metis grinned. "Did Bones and Calypso serve under Captain Hartigan?"

"Bones did," said Ginger. "Strolled up in a tavern, all kitted out in brand-new leathers and won a place on the crew by beating Hobsbawn in a fist fight. Got himself voted as quartermaster in his first three months, the charming galoot."

"And Calypso?" Not that Metis had the mermaid on her mind *at all.* But learning where their former first mate came from had brought home how much Metis did not know about her.

Bonny Blythe was not the only one keeping secrets in their crew.

"Nah, not until… wait!" said Ginger, stumbling to her feet. "Grab 'em while that shrub is blocking the view."

Together they seized Sal, dragging them back over the dunes until the crest of the sandy hillocks hid them from sight of the beach. Metis waved the blue flower in front of Sal's face, hoping for the best. When it didn't have immediate effect, Ginger's hand came around to grind the flower against Sal's nose.

Sal sneezed, and coughed, struggling free of them both. "What is wrong with ya bounders?"

Ginger arched her eyebrows and pointed at the bowtie. "Right back at you, lovely."

Sal stared down at themselves in dawning horror. "Did we go undercover at a butler convention?"

"No, darling, that was just you." Ginger's voice was warm with relief.

Metis scooped up the blue flower from where it had fallen on the sand. It looked rather crushed, but even as it fell apart in her hand, the flower glowed and separated into two perfect-again blooms.

Ginger blinked. "Did that flower…"

Metis tucked one blue flower into her hair, and handed the other to Ginger. "Now we're getting somewhere."

They freed two more crew from the *Caliban* next. Tigris and Elphiny were the current cabin sprats, merry-eyed scamps who had likely lied about their age before donning trousers and running away to sea.

The two girls had wandered away from the group, clearly bored with the hen party. They were easy pickings for the Forget-me-not Brigade.

"We shouldn't rescue Rafferty yet," decided Sal as the five of them clustered behind some trees, further up the dunes from the seashell palace revels. "He's not going to be up for a long walk with his leg, and the maenads might notice if their refreshments stop arriving."

"I'm sure the island would supply them with a new chef," said Metis. "It seems to be making all the decisions around here."

Ginger looked at her with alarm. "I thought it was the Queen behind all this chaos. The local queen, I mean. The one with the hunt."

"Queen Ianthe," Metis murmured. Calypso's mother.

"But you think it's the island in charge, not her?"

"I could punch an island," considered Tigris.

"Like to see you try," snorted Elphiny.

"I still haven't seen the Queen," remarked Metis. "At least, I don't think I have?"

Ginger shuddered. "You wouldn't mistake her for anyone else, love. The Queen of the Isle of Dream doesn't have a head."

The sea witch wore a streaming teal silk cape, and had no head upon her neck — her head was mounted on a staff which she raised in triumph, rattling the long grey braids…

"Wait," said Metis, shaking her head as if that would make it easier to picture the memory. "Is that true? Queen Ianthe doesn't have a head?"

"The Queen's hunt was barmy," enthused Tigris.

"Barking," Elphiny agreed. "I rode a monster with ears bigger than my elbows!"

"You rode me down," Tigris accused, applying a pointy elbow to Elphiny's ribs. "Captured me."

"I never did!" They scuffled together.

"Wonderful!" broke in a refined, painfully aristocratic voice.

Metis around, and into the warm brown eyes of her own queen, who still — thank goodness — had her head.

Aud of the Teacup Isles stood barefoot on the sand, as sweet and serene as if she was hosting a garden party. Her gown — a gauzy, scandalous white garment that belonged in the sort of opera about nymphs and fauns that Mamma would never have let Metis attend until her fortieth birthday, and perhaps not even then — was torn in various places, revealing soft brown curves usually covered up by a great deal more fabric. Her ripped garment was smeared with sea salt, stained with wine.

Beside Queen Aud stood Mneme, Metis' sensible and ladylike cousin, likewise garbed in ripped white cotton, her red hair a wild pile of knots and tangles. On the other side of Queen Aud: the monstrous figure of a manticore.

Sphinx-like shape, a lion's body paired with the whipping tail of a scorpion, and the face…

Metis had never seen a manticore before. She was certain they were not supposed to exist. In storybooks, they were generally the colour of, well, lions and scorpions. Not bold shades of teal and purple as if someone had popped by with a new set of oil paints and the artist couldn't resist.

His face was human. Metis knew that manticores of legend were supposed to have human faces, but most tapestries and vintage illustrations tended to leave out that detail, as it was rather disturbing.

It was disturbing now. Metis *knew* that face. Trapped in the body of a lion and a scorpion was the grumpiest client that the privateers of the *Caliban* had ever had the misfortune to work for.

Lord Manticore. The queen's lover (according to rumour) as well as her official Advisor in Magical Matters. One of the most powerful magisters in the Teacup Isles, and the Isle of Dream had turned him into a royal steed… or a pet.

It would have been funny if it were not utterly horrifying.

"I'm so glad you're here," said Queen Aud, her eyes dazed. "Let me introduce you to our hostess. Queen Ianthe is longing to see you."

"That's all right," Ginger blurted. "Don't mind us, we're on our way…"

Metis wanted to spring forward, to push the bright blue flower under her cousin's nose, not to mention the queen's, but something stopped her. Her feet felt as if they were buried in the sand, melted into glass. "Mneme," she whispered.

Mrs Mneme Seabourne smiled a chilling smile that did not belong to her. It did not belong anywhere near her. "You're just in time, my dears! We're about to play croquet. Such fun."

∼

Croquet was a useful pastime for ladies, in the Teacup Isles. Metis had always preferred it to dancing — she preferred to be outdoors, after all. Croquet was one of the more active courting rituals, as the game allowed you to demonstrate your magical accomplishments in all manner of creative ways. Nothing was off the table: a clever player could transform her opponent's hoop just before she hit her ball, or change the ball itself into something the wrong shape to play through. Sticks became ostrich feathers, balls became cushions or hedgehogs, hoops became cream cakes or adders or bunches of daffodils.

It occurred to Metis, trudging along the sand towards the towering, empty shapes of the Seashell Palace, that her habit of pouring excess magic into the hull and deck of the *Caliban* had been refined on the croquet lawn as much as the embroidery hoop. Her stick had always been harder than anyone else's, and resistant to the charms of others.

After her own chilly childhood, Metis' first instinct was always to protect.

Mneme was older than Metis. She was the one who got things right while Metis inevitably failed at everything that Seabourne ladies were supposed to accomplish: magic, elegance, the right sort of marriage. But now something horrible was happening to Mneme, and *Metis* could save her. She just had to walk a little closer, press the blue flower against her cousin's nose and mouth…

"New guests," said a voice that crackled with magic. "What fun."

Metis blinked. Standing before the Seashell Palace, her bony hand resting on the neck of a bright green water dragon, was a sea witch.

There was no denying who or what she was. Queen Ianthe was tall, skin as pale as sea-foam, glowing with brittle, ageless beauty. Her hair was a matted tangle of braids (silver and gold now, rather than the grey Metis had seen during the hunt), decorated with jewelled bones and tiny gilded skulls. Her gown was a wide-hipped museum piece, like something Grandmamma might have worn when she was young, all padding and upholstery and likely genuine whalebone from a creature she had hunted with a spear.

Queen Ianthe's left arm was covered with the whorl of a tattoo — Metis had not yet succumbed to the sailor's art, but admired it tentatively on her friends — depicting a shipwreck, three swords, and several drowning skeletons.

Utterly terrifying, this woman. Not just a witch of the sea. She had a wiry crown upon her head, studded with pearls.

More pearls in a thick choker around her neck.

Is that what's keeping her head on her shoulders? Metis thought wildly. Last time she had seen that head, it was on the end of a staff — the same staff that the sea witch now held in her right hand.

"We are honoured to introduce," said Mneme, making a courtly curtsey.

"The Queen of the Isle of Dream," said Queen Aud, curtseying even deeper.

"Mistress of this domain."

"Mother of the ocean."

"None of that, my lovelies," cackled the sea witch, who was also the Queen of Dream *and Calypso's mother, oh, gods, this explained so much.* "We'll have a new queen in charge soon enough." Queen Ianthe reached out and snatched at Aud's hand, drawing her into her side.

Metis caught a whiff of old oysters and rum, which did nothing good to her stomach.

"Soon, this precious girl will marry my boy Orion!" announced Queen Ianthe. "We'll have a new mistress to keep this island on the straight and narrow, won't we, my gems?"

The wine-stained, sand-encrusted, swaying ladies all cheered, though few of them looked like they had any idea what she was actually saying.

"Why?" said a sudden voice, sharp and angry. "Can't you control the island yourself, mother?"

The sea-witch hissed between pointed teeth. The crowd murmured. Ginger slid her hand into Metis' and squeezed it wildly.

Calypso approached on bare feet. She now wore a bright green gown covered in a pattern of mermaid scales — the same dress, surely, she had worn on the *Hortensia*, more than a year ago when she smiled at Metis and stole her heart.

She wasn't smiling now.

"You," said Queen Ianthe. "Haven't you done enough?"

"I'm not the one who stole a bride for my son," said Calypso, eyes narrowed.

"And why did I need an heir?" her mother lashed back. "Eight daughters, and you all ran away. "You don't want to be Queen of this Isle."

"No," said Calypso sharply. "I don't. But of all your daughters, I am the only one who returned when you asked for help. Let me find a solution that isn't *this*."

Queen Ianthe's hand flew to her neck. "If you want to help, darling daughter, you can start by finding out who murdered me."

Her fingers tore at the pearls around her neck. As the pearls fell, scattering loosely on the sand, the Queen's head fell too…

LULLED IN THESE FLOWERS
WITH DANCES & DELIGHTS

The air was warm and smelled of flowers. Metis was wearing a dress.

Metis was wearing a *dress*. Not just any old dress. Deep blue satin, with a wispy white shawl draped across her shoulders to mimic sea foam. When she touched her blue hair, she found it arranged impossibly high on her head, like the wig she had been wearing the night she met Calypso. As she reached higher, she found the prow of an ornamental galleon, perched atop the outrageous confection.

The situation was bad enough already, and now Metis had to face it without trousers.

The walls were gold and mirrored here. So many mirrors. Where there was not gold or mirrored glass, there were bright flowers in impossible shades, growing out of the walls.

The music rose and fell, echoing like they were inside a cave instead of yet another…

"Is this another palace?" exclaimed Ginger, at Metis' elbow. "How many palaces does one island need?" She was also gowned in glamour, though this was less of a contrast with her daily attire than it was for Metis: lips dark with crimson, her trademark ginger hair hand-curled and pinned with bones, a bold gown of black and red bombazine, bunched in flattering places and trimmed with silver skulls. A pirate's ballgown.

This was a small antechamber, or possibly the opening passage to a mirror maze. They could hear people nearby — music and dancing and chattering and all the hallmarks of a Society Ball.

Exactly the sort of thing Metis had run away from. "Do I still have my flower?" she asked, rounding on the nearest mirror to examine her reflection.

Oh. She looked beautiful. How unnecessary. Even her freckles had been painted away, as if she hadn't spent the last year of her life working on the deck of a ship in blazing sunlight.

"I don't see it," said Ginger, budging up to admire her own gown in the mirror. "Your hair looks amazing."

"Yes," sighed Metis. "Ominous, isn't it?"

Her blue hair, high and perfect under its golden galleon decoration, with a single curling tendril sliding down her neck, looked as if it had been attended by seventeen ladies-in-waiting or twelve fairy godmothers, whichever came first.

There was no sign of the giant forget-me-not Metis had borrowed from Calypso. Ginger's was gone, too.

"So much for that lifeline."

"We'll just have to fight that sea witch the old fashioned way, like in ballads," said Ginger, squeezing her hand. "Swords, saucy banter and spitting in the eye of fate."

Metis heaved air into her own lungs. "You make it sound entirely achievable. Let's dance."

They found their way out of the glass ante-chamber and into a ballroom also made of glass and crystal, edged with gold. There were staircases, balconies and airy paths criss-crossing over their heads, like they were inside an intricate clockwork ornament.

Everyone was here, it seemed. So many familiar faces.

Doc Smedley danced past, in the arms of Gunner Fry. Doc wore a suit the same bright orange colour as the ceiling of his sickbay the Scurvy Hole. His cravat featured so much lace, it could easily have been three cravats.

There was Mneme, her hair once more restored to its usual tidy arrangement, wearing a prettier version of the bright red dress she had worn to Cousin Henry's first wedding (the wedding that ruined Metis' life). Mneme was dancing with her husband Thornbury, who was still garbed like a crazed flower knight, but held his wife's gaze as if he knew exactly with whom he was dancing.

There was Captain Bell of the *Rosalind*, in the arms of Sal of all people, both of them wearing tailored breeches paired with sleeveless shirts that showed off the tattoos adorning their biceps.

So, *they* got trousers.

Queen Aud, her deep brown skin and black curly hair starkly contrasting with her fluffy white ballgown (or wedding dress?) covered in pearls and embroidery, ran barefoot along one of the upper glass galleries, swinging a croquet mallet. Lady Hadderine pursued her, also armed with a mallet.

There were others playing croquet, here and there all over the ballroom. The dancers moved around the players as if they knew they were there — or, more likely, as if they had been enchanted not to interfere with each other.

"I think it's actually worse if it's an island behind all this and not a person," muttered Ginger. "How can an island have such a warped imagination?"

"That's funny," said Metis. "I was just thinking: I've had this dream."

It wasn't exactly the same — the crew of the *Caliban* had been nowhere near her subconscious the first time she dreamed of a ball in a glass house, with croquet and dancing muddled up together.

She remembered waking up in a cold sweat, night after night during Cousin Henry's house party, thinking: *I can't do this any more. I don't want this life.*

The tableau before her was everything that was terrible and wonderful and agonising about the Season, all rolled together. The only thing that could make it worse would be if Mamma marched up to advise Metis about whom she should trick into marrying her.

Metis and Ginger joined the dance, for the sake of not drawing attention to themselves. Somehow they knew all the steps, whirling in complicated patterns around each other — though even Metis, with her intensive training in vintage dances, was certain she had never seen these particular combinations before.

At the far end of the glass ballroom were two gold thrones on a daïs. On the left throne, a sulky boy-child with long green hair sprawled as if this was the most boring thing he had ever seen in his life. His expression reminded Metis of Cousin Henry during his prime sulking years, around ten or eleven years old.

Ianthe, Queen of the Isle of Dream, sat on the other throne. She was resplendent in a gold gown that matched the gilded throne in every detail. Her head, including the long grey braids with their skull and bone decorations, rested in her lap, having a fierce conversation with Calypso, who knelt on the steps of the daïs.

"She looks trapped," said Metis, noting Calypso's unhappy body language. "Do you think this is why she left us?" It had been a long time since she let herself believe that Calypso had disappeared for a good reason, a worthy reason. Now she wondered all over again.

"I still can't believe she came from here," said Ginger. "Calypso never gave off airs like she'd been raised in twenty seven palaces."

"How was it she first joined the crew?" Metis wondered. They hadn't had a chance to finish their conversation before. "You said she wasn't on the *Miranda*."

"Nah, Captain Hartigan retired after the poor old *Miranda* took too much storm damage once too often. Ship was decommissioned. Bones got his captain's hat and brought as many of us over to the *Caliban* as wanted to come. Calypso turned up a few weeks later, during a mission near Scylla and Charybdis."

Scylla and Charybdis referred to a particularly wild and lawless part of the Tourmaline Strait. Metis knew it well — the *Caliban* had sailed there on a memorable adventure earlier in the year. Hotel Charybdis was a high end casino, surrounded by whirlpools and best approached by portal rather than sailing ship. Scylla was a dangerously sharp rock formation that was sometimes a sea serpent.

The crew of the *Caliban* had barely escaped with their lives, which was par for the course in that neck of the ocean.

"Why was she there?" Metis asked.

"No idea," said Ginger in a soft voice. "It's all a blur, so long ago. We got too close to at least three whirlpools, got our hull spanked silly by the sea serpent. And…" She frowned, shaking her head. "I think there were sirens, and

I've no idea how we survived *that*. Calypso joined the crew, after. No one questioned it. She and Bones got cozy, and you know the rest. She was first mate within a year."

"But you don't remember how or why she came aboard."

"The captain wouldn't keep secrets unless it was something important," Ginger said immediately. "We trust him. So we trusted her."

Metis frowned. That was all well and good, assuming Bones himself remembered. Had Calypso tricked her way into his heart back then, just like she used that seashell to lure the *Caliban* to this island?

"She's Calypso," said Ginger with a shrug. "Whatever happened back in the day doesn't matter. She's one of us now. She gave you the flower, didn't she? That means she's still on our side."

I only knew her for five months; less than half my time on the Caliban. Why is she still so much in my thoughts? How is it the ship still feels wrong without her?

"I think," Metis said softly, her eyes drawn back to the golden thrones. "That might mean we're on *her* side."

"No question," said Ginger, staunchly loyal.

They moved through the dancing couples, propelled in the direction of the golden thrones. As the music came to a brief pause, Metis spiralled out of Ginger's arms and almost collided with Calypso, who was in the process of storming away from her mother.

They stared at each other. Calypso looked unreasonably startled, as if she had not expected Metis to be here.

"Do you need a rescue?" Metis blurted.

Calypso laughed bitterly. "I wish it was that easy."

They did not have time to exchange more words than that, because glass shattered over their heads. So much glass. The air filled with the sound of groaning and cracking. Metis ducked her head, and Calypso pushed her down on to the floor…

She knew she shouldn't look, recognising the danger of a glass palace shattering around them, but Metis had to see what was happening…

Shielding her eyes with one hand, she peeked up just in time to see Captain J. Willoughby Bones riding through the walls of the glass palace upon the back of a giant hedgehog that was also made of glass.

Lillit, Hobsbawn and Damon, returned to their human-sized bodies, clung to the back of the same giant glass hedgehog, waving swords and screaming like they were about to board the enemy.

"Oh…" breathed Calypso, very close to Metis' ear. She moved away, and swore like the sailor she was. "I didn't want to have to do this."

"Do what?" Metis yelled above the noise.

High up over their heads, the balconies and staircases were crumbling and cracking, raining shards of glass down upon the crowd.

Warm fingers slid into Metis' own, as Calypso took her hand and then tossed back her beautiful, golden hair.

Calypso sang.

Time slowed.

The falling glass became flower petals, so many flower petals, blue on blue on blue. Metis felt them on her face, soft and stinging with magic. A deep, old magic that felt entirely familiar, though she could not put her finger on why…

The flower petals weren't the only thing that was falling. Metis tipped backwards, through the floor, and the crew of the *Caliban* fell with her.

SEA-NYMPHS HOURLY RING HIS KNELL

One moment Metis was falling, and the next she was pressed against ancient decking-planks that barely smelled of the sea, with the weight of several squirming bodies heavy on her back.

There was a scramble, and a few barked orders that were oddly comforting because they came from her captain, and finally the crew of the *Caliban* had all climbed off each other. They were still close, huddled on the ground in a loose jumble together, but no one was squashing the breath out of anyone else.

"Sound off," said Bones in a low, urgent voice. "Captain!"

"First Mate!" reported Sal.

"Quartermistress," said Ginger, and so they went all through the ranks until the cabin sprats had called their names.

There was a moment's pause and Calypso said: "and guest," sounding half amused and half wrecked.

Bones huffed out a sigh of relief. He was at Metis'

shoulder and she never wanted him to move any further away. "That's all of us."

"No one from the *Rosalind*," said Ginger, glancing around.

"It was a very specific portal charm," admitted Calypso.

Ginger gave her a wary look. "You brought us here?"

The rest of the crew shuffled around a little, staring at their former first mate in the dim light.

'Here' was full of question marks. Another palace, this one with crumbling stone walls and arched windows far above their heads, allowing moonlight to filter down through lenses of cerulean and amber.

Half of one wall had caved in, collapsed into rubble.

The floor felt like the deck of a ship. There were odd shapes protruding here and there from the walls, as if a ruined palace had grown like mould around the broken pieces of a sailing ship, and then been abandoned for hundreds of years to think about what it did.

"We'll be safe here for a while," said Calypso. "He hates coming to this particular palace." She stood up, stretching her legs, and moved towards a doorway that still had the hinges left upon it, though the door itself was nothing but splinters.

"Where's here?" asked Gunner Fry.

"Who's the *he* you're worried about?" asked Sal.

"I promise," said Calypso. "I'll answer all of your questions." She ducked through the doorway, leaving them with no choice but to follow.

The next room opened out into a cavernous space — with literal cavern rock forming one wall, morphing into square mortared stones on the next, and a giant, curved wooden hull for a third. Half of a bronze name plate disappeared into the deck, swallowing the end of a word that began *PROSPER-*

Torches burst into flame along the walls, one after the other, as the crew mates sidled into the space.

A fountain decorated with marble dolphins adorned the centre of this grand hall. A spiralling stone channel leading away from the fountain, transporting water through another arched doorway. Tiny peach-coloured fish swam here and there in the channel, which looked remarkably clean considering it was being piped through a ruin of a palace that was also, somehow, a shipwrecked vessel.

Calypso climbed up on to the fountain, wedged herself between two marble dolphins, and dipped her bare feet in the water. She was wearing an over-sized white shirt, belted, with bare legs, but the legs didn't last long. They shimmered, transforming into the thick green tail Metis had seen before.

The rest of the crew — all except Bones — were surprised by this, muttering and elbowing each other. Metis glanced up at her tall captain and saw his face steady, his dark eyes giving little away. "What did you want to tell us, Calypso?" Bones asked.

Calypso's tail twitched a little, flicking droplets of water up into the air. "Everything," she promised, her ocean eyes large and luminous. "These are truth fish. I can't lie to you while I'm touching this water."

"That seems convenient," Bones remarked.

Calypso laughed, her voice rich and warm. "Believe me, as someone who grew up on this island, it can be the very opposite."

"Who is this 'he' you want to hide from?" Metis blurted. There were so many questions to ask, but she wanted to get that one in first.

Her question started a cascade.

"What happened to this ship and why is it a palace now?" put in Sal.

"Why are there so many palaces?" was Ginger's question.

"Are you a princess?" asked one of the cabin sprats. "Or not a princess?"

"What's wrong with the magic on this island?" put in Doc Smedley.

"Who changed our clothes?" demanded Lillit.

That question caused another round of muttering. They were indeed all dressed in new clothes, very different to what most of them had been wearing in the glass ballroom. They looked like the cast of *The Good Ship Jolly Roger*, a popular stage musical: all stripes and kerchiefs, unnecessary eyepatches and hooks. Metis was glad to be wearing trousers again, but she would never have chosen to match them with a red striped shirt, nor to bunch her blue hair in pigtails. At least her hair felt the right length again, not nearly long enough to pin up in one of those fancy ballroom arrangements.

Calypso put up her hands in surrender. "No more, give me a chance! Where to begin?" She took a deep breath, preparing to answer her own question.

CALYPSO'S STORY

Twelve years ago, the magister came to our shores. He has many names, but I've always called him the Riddle. He sailed on the pirate ship *Prosperity*. They were wrecked off the coast, thanks to the usual combination of siren song, jagged rocks, and this island's distaste for visitors.

I knew nothing about the magister then except that he

hated the ocean, and our island, and yet he never showed any sign of wishing to leave. Instead, he convinced my mother — the most powerful sea witch of twelve generations — that he loved her, and she loved him in return.

At first it seemed harmless enough, even romantic. They had a son together, my brother Orion.

The Riddle realised soon enough that while she loved him, my mother would never share her power with him. Even if she wanted to, the island would not let her. Our island has always been ruled by queens, and will accept no other ruling hand.

The Riddle took the Summer Palace for his own, drew magic out of the ground and air, and the island hated that most of all — it turned on all of us, until our magic grew stale and our voices weak.

One by one, my sisters left, driven away by the Riddle's greed and our mother's selfish indulgence. There are eight of us in all — daughters of the ocean. We were never princesses, though our mother is a queen. We are sea nymphs, sea witches, mermaids, sirens. Creatures of feather, scale and salt. Some of my sisters have daughters, but they left, too.

Even me, in the end. I could not stay to watch my mother's descent into… well, you've seen her. She wasn't always *that* kind of sea witch. But trying to please the magister and the island at the same time has driven her — I don't know if you'd call it mad. She embraced chaos, and she never found her way back.

I couldn't save her from the magister except by deposing her as queen — and if I did that, I really would be stuck here forever. So I left the island for a new life.

My brother is a prince because our mother made him heir to spite the island. I believe the Riddle still believes my brother can inherit and the Isle of Dream will finally accept a King to rule over it. That is the only explanation for the curse...

~

Calypso paused, looking dizzy. "I haven't answered all your questions. Let me see. Making new palaces is something the island does, all the more so when it's upset. This one — which used to be a plain stone ruin — was created in vengeance against the Riddle when he took the Summer Palace. That's why the *Prosperity* was absorbed into its design. I believe this particular round of costume changes might be because the island sees us as pirates, which isn't good. The island hates pirates." She blinked, and looked around. "What else?"

The sprats both opened their mouths, and Sal clapped a hand around each. "Take a breath," the first mate said calmly.

There was a long pause as the crew of the *Caliban* took in all that Calypso had revealed.

"So, your ma's head is not attached to her body," said Rafferty slowly. "What's up with that?"

Someone kicked him.

"It's a fair question," Calypso said, holding up one hand. "I don't mind. The day I left you..." She stopped and swallowed. Metis felt a warmth press against her hand, as if Bones wanted to hold it, but then he moved slightly away. "I'd always known that if she sent for me, I'd come home. I thought I'd have more time. But earlier this year, my mother sent word to all her daughters that she was dying from a curse. I was the only one who came back. To find the island a mess, our people gone, and my mother... I don't know how she's stayed alive so long. The island must be aiding her, to thwart the magister."

"This magister is the one who took her head off?" said Bones abruptly.

Calypso nodded. "He's proud of it." She looked miserable. "All my sisters stayed away. And his —" She choked for a moment, putting her hand to her mouth. "When I came back, he put a hex on me," she said finally. "The truth fish is the only way to break the command to stay silent about it. The Riddle bound me to him, and recently he sent me back into the mortal world to bring him Queen Aud. He's been courting her at a distance all year — proposals, gifts and the like — on behalf of his son. I assume he thinks that if Orion marries a real queen, he can rule as consort if not as king. And the magister can control Orion."

"It didn't have to be us who brought her here," said Bones calmly. "It didn't have to be the *Caliban*."

Calypso met his gaze with her own. "I missed you all so much. But you're right, I never should have —"

Now it was his turn to hold up a hand. He strode away, following the channel of water through to the next cave (or palace hall) beyond.

"Give him a minute," said Metis, when everyone except Calypso looked expectantly at her. "Let him brood."

"He can have two, then you go after him," decided Sal.

Metis had more to say to Calypso. Two minutes wasn't going to be enough. She stepped forward, perching on the edge of the water and trailing her hand in with the truth fish, keeping her distance from Calypso's majestic tail. "You hexed me," she said, finally free of the chokehold on her throat. "On the docks, on the Isle of Manticore. And when I wouldn't pass the charm on to the captain, you got at him directly. That shell around his neck."

"Yes," said Calypso, looking miserable.

"Queen Aud, too. You did something to her."

"I didn't have to. She's been suggestible to his commands since she first touched the bracelet he sent with the proposal. But I… activated her, I suppose. Let her know it was time to come here."

"At the command of this magister?"

"Yes."

Metis knew the pull of magic like that, but it seemed impossible that Calypso, so strong and confident, had surrendered to its pull. "What happens to your mother when Queen Aud marries your brother?" she snapped. Not that the crew of the *Caliban* were going to let that happen. Stopping inappropriate weddings was something Metis had some experience at, and she was sure the rest of them would get the hang of it quickly.

Calypso looked pale, her cheeks washed of all her usual colour here in this ruined palace which felt more like a cave. "If the island accepts Aud as its queen, it won't need my mother any longer. I don't imagine it will help her fight the Riddle's curse after that."

"She'll die."

Tears filled Calypso's eyes. "She died the moment he cursed her. What's happening now is crueller than that."

Another thought occurred to Metis. "You said everyone left. But I met a frog butler who said he'd served you all his life."

"He probably thinks he has. That's what this magic does — it tells a new story in your head about who you are. You've felt it." Calypso glanced around, and the crew nodded.

Only Metis had escaped the island's storybook transformations. Metis and Bones. Was that because of her embroidered protections?

"The frog servants are what's left of the crew of the

Prosperity," Calypso added. "I assume it was the island's vengeance for bringing the magister here."

Metis nodded, and wiped her hand on her breeches. "It's been two minutes," she said abruptly. "Everyone chat amongst yourselves."

No one acted remotely surprised that it was she who went after the captain. Not even Calypso.

Captain Bones had not gone far.

This particular room was even more cave than palace, with the water from the channel trickling down a series of rock pools alongside a staircase of rough-hewn stone.

The captain sat on the edge of one of the pools, his boots beside him and his bare feet dangling in the water where tiny, sparkling peach fish could nibble at his toes. "The boots were too tight," he remarked as Metis approached.

Like the rest of them, Bones was dressed as the parody of a pirate, although in his case it wasn't too far from his usual attire. His black silk shirt was floppier, his leather trousers a tad tighter (if that were possible) and the boots had giant buckles like they belonged to a pantomime cat.

As she passed close to Bones, Metis recognised her black violet embroideries on his back: it was the same shirt, only slightly transformed. Her protections were still there. Good.

She kicked off her own boots — hers were too loose rather than too tight — and pulled out the silly pigtails, letting her blue hair fall naturally to her shoulders. She rolled off the bright striped socks of her pirate attire before joining him at the pool, dipping her bare feet into the water.

Truth fish. It was no stranger than anything else on this island.

They sat together in a pleasant silence for a moment or two. Metis could hear the echoing mutters and occasional laughter of the crew not far away, their voices bouncing off the broken walls of the ruined palace.

It felt right, to have them all safe and under one roof, even if it wasn't the right roof. Even if that roof was full of holes.

I miss our ship.

Her feet tingled. Metis found truthful words rising up inside her, even without questions to prompt them. "When I was a child I wanted to run away and live in a ruin," she said. "It was the fashion for every big estate to build false ruins in their gardens, so I'd seen plenty of them. Temples, towers… I wanted to live somewhere away from…" She clamped her lips tightly before anything else spilled out.

Metis darted a look at Bones, whose eyes were nothing but warm. "That's the most you've ever told me about yourself," he observed.

"My name isn't Bonny Blythe," she blurted next. "I got it out of a book."

He laughed then, his shoulders rolling easily. "I know. I was a child, once. I read books."

"You know?" Her thoughts were racing. He had read the Bonny Blythe books. "Does *everyone* know?"

The captain shrugged, as if it was no matter. "My original name isn't J Willoughby Bones. You're not the only one who ran away to sea."

"I never said I ran away," Metis said quickly.

He raised his eyebrows. "You were already running, back on the *Hortensia*. When Calypso invited you to jump aboard with us, you didn't even pause."

It had never occurred to her that the captain might

have given any thought to where she came from, or why she chose his ship. "You don't mind?"

Bones scoffed. "Friends don't ask friends about why they choose to tattoo a shark on one leg and slap on an eyepatch. That's what makes privateers better than people."

"Are we friends?" Metis breathed.

He gave her an odd look. "Aren't we?"

There the truth fish went again, darting at her feet with tingling touches. She should never have taken her boots off. *He didn't ask your name, you don't have to…*

"My name is Metis Hephaesta Ariadne Seabourne," she said.

If anything, the captain's eyes grew warmer. "William Von Trask," he said, and held out a hand. They clasped them together, as if meeting for the first time, and then failed to let go. "My father was the worst person in the world," he said next, his fingers lingering over hers. "He used me as a tool to hurt his enemies." So he had his own confessions to make.

"That's what you ran away from?"

"Yes."

Metis wanted to ask him everything about himself while she had the chance. Was that fair? He didn't seem to object. He could take his feet out of the water any time he liked… "That necromancer?"

"My brother. The spellcracker?"

"Cousin-by-marriage."

"You're one of *those* Seabournes."

She knew exactly what he meant by that. Seabourne women were legendary for their epic magical achievements. Theirs was such an influential and infamous family that most men marrying into it would find it a boon to his career to change his name to Seabourne. Thornbury had, and Mneme's father, and Metis' father… "Yes," she said calmly.

One of those Seabournes could mean a lot of things. It didn't mean he had heard about her mother's disgrace…

"No wonder you were able to save my ship," Bones said, nodding as if it all made sense.

"Why are you being so kind?" Metis demanded. "I've been lying to you since we met. I'm only telling you the truth now because we're paddling with magical fish."

Bones drew his brows together, creasing his forehead. This only served to make him more handsome, which was entirely uncalled for. "Really," he said, his voice as gravelly as the rock pool around them. "You can't think of a single reason?"

Metis kissed him.

She had wanted for so long to feel his mouth on hers. It had been an idle fantasy, nothing she actually thought could *happen*, not even after Calypso broke his heart. Bones had only started to feel like a person rather than a captain since they landed on these shores, and nothing was real here anyway.

If nothing was real, she could kiss him and it wouldn't matter.

Might as well make it a good one. Her hands tangled against his shirt, pulling him into her. No need to be a lady about it.

Bones took control of the kiss, as if it had been his idea in the first place. He buried one hand in Metis' hair at the nape of her neck and opened his mouth to hers.

Heat and thrill rushed through her. Together they explored, lips on lips, a moment of rough tongue, until finally they broke apart.

"I'm still in love with Calypso," Bones blurted, and immediately looked like he wanted to stab himself.

(Their feet were still in the pool with the truth fish.)

Metis let out a short, strangled laugh. "So am I," she admitted when she could breathe again.

They stared at each other, eyes wide. No secrets left.

Around them, the walls began to shake.

Calypso appeared in the archway from the other cave. She had legs again, her toes bright pink under the damp hem of her over-sized white shirt. "He's coming!" she yelled. "The Riddle. We have to get out of here!"

"You said this was safe," Bones snapped up at her, helping Metis out of the pool. Quickly, not looking at each other, they put their boots back on.

"He never comes here, I don't know how…"

Something had been gnawing at Metis. "Calypso," she interrupted. "Why do you call him the Riddle?"

"It's nothing," said Calypso, motioning them back through the caves. "Come on! Just a stupid nickname to annoy him. Make him seem smaller than he was."

"But why *that* nickname?" Metis pressed.

"Because he hates the ocean," Calypso said wildly. "He sailed on a pirate ship to steal our home and he hates it, he hates that there's nowhere on this island you can't smell the sea."

"Can we do this later?" Bones asked, impatient with both of them.

"That's not a riddle," Metis insisted, at Calypso's heels as they hurried to join the others. "Unless…"

She wanted to be wrong. It was a sickening, dreadful possibility. She wished she hadn't thought of it at all.

"Because of his name," said Calypso. She raised her hands in the air. With a casual use of magic that almost knocked Metis flat on the ground, Calypso conjured a portal in the ceiling above. The portal glimmered like a rainbow, pale and perfect. Music emanated from it, the sound of singing like a thousand sea nymphs and sirens had returned to save their island. "He never uses it, it's not even funny, it just always put him on edge him to remind him where he came from…"

"Calypso!" Metis yelled over the din. "What's the magister's name?"

"Seabourne," said Calypso, as if the word meant nothing to her. She lowered her hands, and the portal yawned down to swallow the entire crew of the *Caliban*.

THE MAGISTER

WHAT CARE THESE ROARERS
FOR THE NAME OF QUEEN?

etis hit sand, her memories tumbling over and over. *Seabourne*. A tall, stern man with a shock of red hair. A commanding voice, a shrug, a door slamming in her face…

She became aware of shouts and hollers around her. Dawn's rosy fingers were coming over the horizon, and her crew had finally been reunited with their *Caliban*. She couldn't look, couldn't share the crew's joy or join their chaotic plans to tip their ship back upright, get her back on the water.

The sand was hot and gritty under her fingers.

Seabourne.

"Blythe." Her captain loomed over her for a moment, and then he knelt in front of her on the sand, holding her hand between his own. Large. Comforting. "Metis," he said, speaking her name quietly, so no one else could hear. "Are you —" There was a question he didn't finish.

She had told him her name. Thanks to the truth fish, Bones knew what it meant that Calypso's riddle of a magister was called Seabourne.

"My father Gaulliver left home twelve years ago, and never returned," she said now, her voice shaky. "He was a powerful magister, and…" Cruel. Intelligent. Ambitious. "He hated the ocean," she said, and began to laugh a little.

Was it a surprise that her father had spent more than a decade on an isolated island, hating the place while trying to bend its magic to his will?

Not in the least. Gaulliver Seabourne had too much pride to admit to such a mistake.

"You should be with your crew," she said half-heartedly, trying to push her captain away. "Your ship…"

"*You're* my crew," Bones said, eyes on hers.

"Your father," broke in Calypso, closer than Metis had realised.

Metis looked up in a panic and saw the mermaid standing barefoot and bare-legged on the sand in that over-sized shirt of hers, watching them both with her thoughtful ocean eyes.

For a moment, Metis thought Calypso was going to say something more about her father, or about the fact that Bones was still holding her hand, but Calypso had more urgent concerns. "You have to go. All of you. Get out of here while you can."

Metis considered it. She longed to be back on the *Caliban*, the salt air in her face. She could practically hear the sails unfurling and the crew climbing about on the ropes. Off on their next adventure…

She stood up in a rush, dragging Captain Bones with her. "What are you talking about? We can't leave."

Calypso hugged herself, looking miserable. "You must."

"Without Queen Aud?" Without Mneme and Mr Thornbury, or the crew of the *Rosalind*, or Bones' evil necromancer brother?

Bones stood behind Metis, his right hand wrapped

around her right hand, his left hand resting on her left shoulder. "We're not done here, Calypso."

For a moment, Calypso's eyes flashed gold. "I can make you leave."

Bones still wore the golden seashell so yes, she probably could, though Metis had some idea of how to thwart her. The crew of the *Caliban* could be stirred to mutiny in a good cause, if their bosun told them that the captain had been enchanted by malign forces. (According to ship gossip this happened on average once a year, so he was overdue.)

"What happens?" the captain said fiercely. "If we sail away and leave this mess behind?"

"The Queen of the Teacup Isles marries a ten-year-old," Metis said. *Oh, gods. I have a brother.* "Which is exactly what the magister wants. You're still working for him, Calypso."

Calypso opened her mouth and choked on air as the curse silenced her. Gaulliver Seabourne's curse.

"It's not your fault," Metis added, more gently. "But we can't trust a word you say."

Her father had cast a speak-not charm on Metis once, when the noise of his daughter playing with the children next door offended his ears. He left it on her for three months, only removing it because he wanted her to pass on a sarcastic message to her mother about the butcher's bill, and he couldn't find a pen.

"Do you think the magister's seashell is why you and I haven't been affected by the island's tricks?" Bones asked Metis, his voice close to her ear as he turned over her hand and brushed his thumb over the seashell mark that still bruised her palm.

"Those are our royal seals," Calypso said, sounding brittle. "They're not his to use."

"And yet he uses them." Bones turned his dark eyes on

her. "Unless you sent the courting gift to Aud of the Teacup Isles? This Seabourne usurped your seals and your family name. As if he was this island's king." Bones squeezed Metis' hand, offering what comfort he could.

The sand underneath their feet shifted. Clearly the island did not like the idea of the magister having such power.

Maybe the island should have done something about this years ago, if the magister's plans were so objectionable. Had the queen's love protected him, as long as it lasted?

"Why not you?" Metis asked Calypso. "My — this magister wants power, so he married a queen. That didn't work, so he sent you off into the world to find another queen to marry his son. But that's not what the island wants." As she spoke, she felt the sand shiver again. The sky, even as it lightened with the sunrise, closed over with rainclouds. She was getting close to the answer. "You're the daughter of the Queen of the Isle of Dream. None of your sisters came home when she called for help, only you. Why aren't you the heir?"

Calypso stared at Metis, mouth open in shock as if she had said something awful.

For the first time since they arrived on the Isle of Dream, it began to rain. Not just rain. It bucketed down. Cold and wet and shocking, all at once.

Bones and Metis did not move, staring at the mermaid they both loved.

"Cap'n," called Sal from somewhere. "She might be the wrong way up, but we can shelter in the ship."

Bones held up a hand. "Don't wait for us!"

"If you were a queen," Metis went on, relentlessly, despite the terrible look on Calypso's face that told her *stop*, stop pushing. "The island would be happy. You could achieve what your mother never did, and finally banish the magister from your domain. The magic would heal. Perhaps your people would come back — your sisters. Your family. Everyone who left because of him. Why wouldn't you want that?"

Calypso put both hands to her mouth, shaking her head wildly. Her golden hair had been beaten into thin strands by the angry rain.

"You'd be trapped here," Bones guessed. His voice was steady. His hand was the only warmth that Metis could feel. "The Queen of the Isle of Dream could never return to the *Caliban*."

Calypso's hands fell away. "I knew when I left the ship that it would be forever. I don't deserve your forgiveness."

"Why not?" Bones asked, his voice soft enough it could barely be heard over the rain.

"I've been lying to you since we met. About everything I ran away from."

Bones squeezed Metis' hand once more. "We're all runaways. Why didn't you tell me what was happening — your mother's curse, the summons to return home? Did you think I wouldn't understand?"

"You'd have tried to help," Calypso said plaintively.

"We're trying to help now." Bones was doing his best to be patient with her, but patience had never been his strong point.

"I should never have involved you," Calypso said explosively. "That was a stupid impulse because I missed you all, I was trying to rebel against —" Again, she choked on air. She still couldn't speak of Gaulliver Seabourne without the aid of the truth fish. "I didn't want you here. I didn't want our beautiful ship to — do you know how many ships have been wrecked on these shores? The Isle of Dream is home to mermaids and sirens and sea witches, and most of us might be related, but we're not a *family*.

We're the opposite of a crew. We ruin everything. I never wanted to pick pieces of the *Caliban* off our sand."

"Look at her, she's fine!" Bones raised his voice now, either because of the noisy rain or because he was finally losing his temper. "She made it to the beach in one piece. Blythe held the hull together."

Calypso gave him an inscrutable look. Her eyes darted to where he was still holding Metis' hand. "And what about you, Captain Bones?" she asked in a broken voice.

"She held me together too."

Calypso burst into tears.

Metis reached her first, wrapping her arms around the neck of the sobbing mermaid, kissing her cheek. Bones was close behind, his arms coming around both of them. "We will fix this," he said, sounding rough but determined. "We will get you out of this. And Queen Aud, and everyone else."

"You can't save everyone!" Calypso howled into his neck.

"Watch me."

Metis pressed her face against the soft curve of Calypso's shoulder. They were wet and cold and miserable, but they were together and surely, *surely* there was an answer.

"What if I have to become Queen to save everyone?" Calypso asked in a sob.

Bones laid his forehead against hers. "Then you'll be in the market for privateers, won't you? I warn you, we're choosy bastards. We only work for royalty."

The galley of the *Caliban* was on its side, pots and pans everywhere. Somehow, Rafferty had managed to light the stove and put a brew on. The crew were squashed in together with tin mugs of tea when their captain, bosun and former first mate joined them. The mingling scents of Unicorn Tears, Siren Song and Queen of Tides filled the stuffy cabin.

Captain Bones shook droplets from his long dark hair, which had started to come loose from its braiding. Doc Smedley, currently squeezed on to a bench with Gunner Fry on his lap, reached over and cast a drying charm on him.

Metis cast one over herself before Smedley had the chance, and offered it to Calypso who gave a wan smile and dried herself between one eye-blink and another. "A mermaid thing."

"There have been some developments," said the captain, accepting a mug as drinks were passed across. "We're caught between two powers: the magister Seabourne, and this island."

"Which side are we on?" Sal asked.

"Our side," Captain Bones growled. "There is no other."

"There's a problem," Metis said quietly. "The island can control you — that's why you all kept forgetting who you were, changing identities, playacting different roles." She indicated herself, Bones and Calypso. "And we —" Her throat tightened, and she coughed on dust.

"Let me guess," said Doc Smedley with narrowed eyes. "The magister has a taste for golden seashells."

Metis gave him a weak smile, flashing him the seashell mark on her palm. "I don't think he can have any sway over me, thanks to your work. The same can't be said for these two. But it still seems to be protecting me from the island's influence." Unless it was the violets.

Smedley nodded. "Does he know about you, this magister Seabourne?"

"I don't know. I don't think he knows who I am, at least," Metis added. Then, with a quick glance at Calypso. "Unless you told him?"

Calypso gave her a weak smile and nudged her shoulder. "*I* didn't know who you were."

Metis turned back to the rest of the crew, who all put on innocent faces like they weren't dying to know. "My real name is Metis Seabourne," she said heavily. "That probably doesn't mean anything to you. But I think this magister is my father."

"Doesn't mean anything?" the cabin sprat Tigris scoffed. "We read newspapers, bosun."

"I remember that one," Elphiny put in eagerly. "The old Seabourne hag tried to use magic to force a hot duke into marriage, and they locked her in the Tower of…"

Bones glared at her. "On this ship, Bosun Blythe does not need to be reminded of her family or her past. Which is a courtesy everyone enjoys."

Tigris and Elphiny both looked mortified. "Sorry," they muttered.

Damon raised a hand. "So is the wedding still happening, my loves?"

"We spent half the night running around after that prince on his stag do," Lillit added. "Which is weird now I think about it. He's barely old enough to be a cabin sprat."

"We're going to stop the wedding," said Metis.

"I'm not sure we can," put in Calypso.

Metis turned and glared at her. "He's a child. And Queen Aud is under magical influence. It's not right."

Calypso shook her head. "The magister wants it to happen. He always gets what he wants."

Metis stood firm. "He has been trying and failing to rule this island for a decade. I think he can take a little more disappointment." She had never got a chance to rebel against her father's cruelty — he left home long before she grew a backbone. She wasn't going to let him hurt her now, or the people she loved.

"The island wants the wedding!" Calypso protested. "This wedding is the only thing they both agree on."

"Well, then," said Metis, thinking of a wedding last year, which had been prevented in the nick of time. "I think it's time to throw some teacups."

Her words were followed by a bemused silence.

"No idea what that means," said one of the sprats. "But it sounds *wicked*."

13

YOU ARE CORDIALLY INVITED

The Summer Palace stood at the very centre of the Isle of Dream — the furthest you could get from the sea on all sides. The magister who hated oceans was consistent.

"This was my favourite palace, when I was a child," said Calypso. "It was the colour of sunshine, and full of flowers."

"Favourite palace," snorted Ginger. "Not a princess, she says," she added in an undertone.

The crew of the *Caliban*, still garbed in their piratical fancy dress, gathered at the edge of a green forest like something out of a dark and mysterious fairy tale, except that the trees were all roughly the height of Sal. Bones, Ginger and other members of the crew who were above average height had to crouch, so as to remain hidden in the foliage.

The Summer Palace was no longer the colour of sunlight. It was tall and wide and grey, with spiky turrets and bleak slitted windows. It was surrounded by a wide courtyard of grey slate flagstones, surrounded by silvery grass, surrounded by this pint-sized dark forest.

If Metis had held any doubt that the Seabourne magister was her father, then no longer. His magic bled into the air, as familiar as her own.

The seashell mark on her hand twinged, like someone had recently stabbed it with a knife.

"Doesn't look like anyone's planning a wedding," Sal observed. "No ale, no cakes. Bit of a washout."

"He'll be holding back until the guests arrive," said Calypso. "For greater effect. When he married my mother, he conjured every sugared almond and orange blossom out of thin air in front of the guests."

Married. Metis blinked several times, absorbing the idea that her father had married again. "My mother's still alive," was the first thing she thought to say. "There was no divorce." Or had there been? Her parents never told her much unless it was a message they wanted the other to hear.

It would be just like Hecate Seabourne to divorce her husband and never say a word about it to her daughter.

Calypso gave Metis a wan smile. "The Isle of Dream cares more about ceremony than paperwork."

"Clearly."

Best not to think about how Metis and Calypso were technically stepsisters, or that they shared a sibling in this Prince Orion. Better not to think too hard about any legalities that might arise from this strange new life her father had stolen for himself…

No, they were here for one task only. To prevent Queen Aud and her child bridegroom from getting married.

Haunting, crooning horns blew out across the silent morning. Several frog butlers marched out of the forest in pale silver-grey morning coats over striped waistcoats and tight white breeches. They blew what looked like enormous conch shells.

(Now Metis came to pay attention, there were clues that the frog butlers had originally been pirates — one of them had a peg-leg and several others wore eyepatches which looked especially strange on the face of a frog.)

The frog butlers were followed by a pageant of familiar faces. The necromancer and the spellcracker, garbed as the purple and yellow flower knights Sir Florimel and Sir Florizel, carried enormous banners covered in golden seashells.

Mneme Seabourne and Lady Hadderine wore long white tunics, less raggedy than during the 'hen party,' decorated with skulls and bones and seed pearls. They both carried baskets of flower petals, hurling handfuls into the air at random intervals.

The privateers of the *Rosalind* followed, wearing similar concoctions of white fabric and flowers. No one wore shoes, which must have made for a tough walk.

Then the beasts of the Queen's hunt, prowling around the perimeter of the Summer Palace, ready to start a siege rather than celebrate a wedding. The multi-coloured manticore was there, as was the giant glass hedgehog.

Queen Aud walked out of the forest with Queen Ianthe at her side. They both wore white tunics and flowers, their legs bare. Calypso's mother was taller, her head returned to her shoulders and her wild, gilded grey braids falling down her back. She held her staff, and wore a high, fragile crown of gilded seashells and woven grass fronds.

Queen Aud, so short and dark compared to the tall, bleached-pale figure of Ianthe, had pinned a gauzy veil over her thick black curls, with a circlet of spiky white flowers over the top. A golden seashell bracelet gleamed on her wrist.

They looked remarkably humble, for a bride and a mother of the bride, let alone two queens. As the crowd parted, Aud and Ianthe knelt on the grass facing the Summer Palace.

Calypso let out a growl. "I want to burn that palace to the ground," she muttered. "And the blasted Riddle with it."

"Don't get ahead of yourself," said Bones, kissing her on the top of her head — an absent gesture, as if he had done it a thousand times. Metis waited to feel jealous about it, and did not. "Cake first, burnings later."

"We might not want to let them get as far as cake," considered Metis. Wedding cakes, in her experience, were not to be trusted.

The seashell horns rang out, higher and louder. The drawbridge of the Summer Palace lowered. The bridegroom and his father emerged.

Tea and cake came with them.

Tray after tray of tiny, exquisite sugared dainties and crustless triangle sandwiches flew out of the Summer Palace, garnished with lush edible flowers and carved fruits. They spun outwards, hovering in the air as a guard of honour between the magister, his son, and their guests.

Teacups, brimming with hot tea, came flying out next, propelled by butterfly wings the same colour as the porcelain — in some cases, matching the china pattern exactly.

Sweet punch came next, crystal bowl after crystal bowl, and a whole array of pretty tumblers.

Jellies: majestic and jewel-coloured, wobbling on silver salvers.

It was a wedding breakfast fit for an army of ravenous

queens. Absurd, but only slightly more so than your average aristocratic picnic at the height of the Season.

He was using so much magic, Metis realised. It was a show of force, a deliberate display of power. Holding all those plates in the air, all those teacups… this was not the island's magic. It was Gaulliver Seabourne, to the bone china.

What an ass her father was. Somehow this had never occurred to Metis — she had come to terms with her mamma's faults over the years, but her father's early exit from their lives had left him something of a mythic figure. Not faultless, but untouchable.

Looking at him now, she felt contempt. What a tedious person, all drama and pointless posturing.

Gaulliver Seabourne wore an old-fashioned suit — he'd hardly had a chance to visit a tailor in the last decade — with professorial magister's robes thrown over the top: black with gold sigils. His hair was a shock of silver; he didn't look old, exactly, but he had certainly aged in the years since Metis last saw him. She remembered his hair being dark like storm clouds. His eyes, though, were bright blue, just like hers. A little too familiar.

She was scared of him, she realised, had been terrified of him for her entire childhood. Not for anything he had done in particular, but for what he might do should he find her annoying, or inconvenient. Standing so near him now, she wondered what all the fuss had been about.

"We need to wait for the right moment," Calypso murmured to Captain Bones.

"No," Metis decided. "I don't think that will be necessary." She broke their cover, walking with determination out of the trees and toward the Summer Palace.

When she reached the perimeter of flying teacups, she lifted one out of the air and held it, dropping a brief swapping charm upon its contents. Nothing elaborate, but the warm tea was instantly exchanged for cold sea water from the beach where the *Caliban* waited for them.

Gaulliver Seabourne, 'the riddle,' the magister who hated oceans, glanced at her in her striped shirt and black boots and bright blue hair, and dismissed her as anyone important. "No pirates were invited to this wedding," he drawled

"Not a pirate," Metis said cheerfully. "I'm a privateer. We're *worse*." She flashed her palm at him, holding the seashell mark. "Does this look familiar?"

Seabourne frowned. "You're with Calypso."

Chance would be a fine thing. "I'm with the *Caliban*," Metis corrected. "Come on out," she called to her crew.

She he heard them muttering behind her as they approached, including one Bones-like mutter in particular, about bosuns getting too big for their britches.

"Your presence is unnecessary," said Gaulliver Seabourne, frowning at Metis like he was trying to place her. "Unless you're here to eat cake and throw rice."

"We're here to take back our queen," said Metis. She'd developed a knack for projecting her voice on the *Caliban*. No point in a polite murmur when there was a squall at sea and a rope needing to be untied right the hell now. Her raised voice carried in a pleasing manner across the hovering tea party, so everyone could hear her.

"You have been misinformed," said Gaulliver Seabourne, radiating smugness. "Queen Aud is about to become *our* queen."

Metis nodded politely. "Let's ask her, shall we?"

Casting embroidery charmwork was second nature to Metis, as easy as breathing — and she'd been practicing ever since she and Bones first set foot on this island. She lifted a hand now, dotting Queen Aud's plain white dress with a series of bright blue flowers.

(Forget-me-nots, so appropriate.)

The magister snarled, lunging at her. Behind her, Metis heard the metallic scrape of Bones and others drawing their swords, but that was not necessary — not when she had just flung a teacup full of seawater into her father's face.

That was another detail she had remembered, raking through old childhood memories as her crew prepared for battle. The reason her father hated the ocean was because his magic worked better away from salt water. Magisters called it a *bane* — a fatal flaw that weakened their magic. It might be a language, a colour, a smell. Some magisters searched for decades and never learned what theirs was. It must have been so frustrating to him that his bane was something commonly found across the Teacup Isles.

And yet he had run away to another small island and tried to rule it. Talk about hubris.

Should have gone to the continent, Metis thought mercilessly, watching her father sputter, seawater dripping down his face.

The cups rattled in their saucers. The floating platters wobbled wildly. Several of them toppled to the grass, but others stayed up.

Queen Aud let out a gasping breath as the magister's magic cracked just enough to give her back her own identity. She stared around at the strange forest and palace and assortment of people. "What is happening? Where is my Manticore?"

"Your Majesty!" Metis called across to her. "We are royal privateers, of your good ship *Caliban*. May we assist?"

Queen Aud's dark eyes arrowed into her. "Why am I here, Miss Seabourne?"

That was the downside of having been presented at court; it was hard to be anonymous, and their Queen had an uncanny memory for faces. Apparently blue hair and trousers did not hamper her in reaching for the right name.

Metis gestured in the direction of Gaulliver. "This magister summoned you to marry a child so that you might replace the queen of this isle. I suggest you remove those golden seashells immediately!"

Queen Aud touched her wrist, and pulled her fingers back as if burned.

"NO!" roared Gaulliver Seabourne. "Stand fast, queen. I give the orders."

Queen Aud struggled for a moment, her hand frozen. Then she unclasped the bracelet in one swift moment. The golden seashells fell to the grass.

I did that, Metis thought in shock and delight. Then: *how did I do that?*

She could feel the magister's power rushing back to him, far too quickly. The air stung with it. She had only earned a brief respite from her teacup of seawater. Should have brought a bucket.

Gaulliver was staring at her, his blue eyes bright. He was so slender, bony under those fancy robes. No wonder she had grown up skinny and strong instead of short and curvy like her mamma.

"Who are you?" he demanded, attention now entirely on Metis, not any of the royals or subjects or sailors around them. "Why do you… that's *my magic*."

She felt him burrowing inside her skin, awful and familiar. He nudged against something she had not even realised was there, like a wax seal imprinted with the name of Gaulliver Seabourne…

Or, as it turned out, like a cork in a barrel.

The magister reared back, pulling his probing magic

with him, but it was too late. His presence had disturbed the spell, and the curse he had placed on his daughter now leaped free, thirsty to be reunited with its master.

Colours swamped the scene, brighter than Metis had ever seen them. Grass was so green, the sky so blue, and when Bones caught her before she fell, she stared into his face wondering how she ever functioned at all when someone so brilliant, so beautiful was in her vicinity.

"What have you done to her?" Calypso cried.

Metis rolled and grasped the tails of Calypso's white shirt to stop her from doing anything stupid. "It was an old wound," she choked. "It — he'll regret that one."

She had always wondered about her magic. She was a Seabourne, after all. They were supposed to be mighty. Her parents were both powerful magisters. Her cousins… Henry was brimming with magic, and like most gentlemen, utterly careless in how he spent it. Mneme, who deliberately played the wallflower for years, kept her charmwork discreet and domestic so as not to call attention to herself.

But *Metis* had always had so little to work with. Her magic was constantly there, an endless supply like a dripping tap. But somehow, though it felt uncomfortable if she went too long without pouring it into something (like her embroideries, or the hull of the ship), it was never available in larger quantities for her to control. Like hearing someone singing from several rooms away.

Now she knew why.

At some point in her childhood — before she was old enough to understand — her father the magister had done something to her magic. Not taking it away — but hiding it where she could not fully reach it or see it or judge how much of it there was.

Mamma must have known. She must have allowed him to do it… unless this was the act that ended all cordiality in their marriage? It would be nice to think so, but then, why would Hecate Seabourne not have done something to thwart her husband's spell over the years? *So many years.*

It must have suited her to keep Metis' magic contained.

It was not contained now. Magic spilled out of her, staining the air with stripes of red and gold and brilliant light. She rose to her feet, accepting Bones' warm hand as it closed around hers. She reached out with her other hand to hold Calypso's, too. Then Miss Metis Seabourne stepped forward to meet her father.

Gaulliver Seabourne looked pale, genuinely worried for himself. When Metis stepped forward, he stepped back. "Daughter," he said, acknowledging her.

Metis swallowed. Her throat was dry, but there was nothing to stop her from speaking. She turned over the hand holding Calypso's and saw that the seashell mark had finally faded from her palm.

"You need to stop," she told him. "This island isn't yours. It doesn't want you. You have wrecked everything you touched here. It's time to go."

"Go?" Gaulliver's voice was incredulous. "I have worked for twelve years to make this island my own. You think I will give it up now, because another bloody Seabourne woman thinks she can tell me what to do?"

(Metis remembered an old argument, before the great silence — her mamma shrieking: "*If my name is such a burden to you, give it back!*" Men who married Seabourne women knew they were taking on a force greater than themselves. It had never occurred to Metis before that some Seabourne husbands might not be up to the challenge.)

Metis felt exhausted. She did not wish to delve further into Gaulliver Seabourne's mind, or learn his motives. She felt no need to pour out her heart-hurts to his face. She was, truth be told, tired of looking at him.

There was more to do — they still had to set the island to rights, rescue Calypso, rescue Queen Aud, rescue Prince Orion, and sail away in the *Caliban* with all hands safe and well.

The day was young. All things were possible.

It was time to get started.

14

NOT FOR THY FAIRY KINGDOM

The air was sweet around the Summer Palace.
Metis, reunited with all her magic for the first
time since childhood, had made up her mind.

Gaulliver Seabourne, her father, the magister who
hated the ocean, stared back at her from behind his
perimeter of flying teacups, waiting for her to make the
first move.

Such a weak man, Metis thought to herself. *The ultimate
land-lubber.*

"Captain Bones," she called behind her.

"Yes, love?" (Love, had he really called her that, or did
she mishear 'Blythe'? No time to wonder.)

"What do privateers do with their prisoners?" she
asked him.

Bones chuckled. "Much like pirates, darling," he said
(*darling*, there was no mistaking that word for anything but
exactly what it was). "We use rope."

Fair enough. Rope was well within Metis' abilities. She
was the bosun of the *Caliban*, and she knew where every

spare canvas, hook and length of rope was in that entire ship. (Even if the ship was still upended on a beach.)

Rope.

Sympathetic magic was an easy go-to for Metis. Do something here, affect something there.

She thought hard about a particular length of rope, coiled up in the hold of the *Caliban*, then she tugged a thread from the cuff of her striped pirate shirt, and tossed it into the air. For a moment, there was silence. Then, behind them, a swishing, whipping sound among the trees.

A ship's rope whipped over the heads of Metis and her crew, smashed several floating teacups, and wrapped itself soundly around the body of Gaulliver Seabourne.

Metis dragged another thread from her cuff and tied it in a quick succession of sailor's knots which replicated themselves upon the ropes binding her father.

"Nice work," breathed Calypso.

Gaulliver's face was twisted in anger now, as he stared at his daughter. The remaining teacups and cakes quivered in the air, barely staying upright.

Metis walked closer. She swept several teacups aside with a flick of her hand. She glanced over at the boy prince (her brother!), who had been standing nearby all this time, either dazed or bored. When Orion saw her looking, the little imp stuck his tongue out at her.

"Why are you even here?" Gaulliver demanded in frustration.

He still didn't know. Had no idea how his own melodramatics and machinations had led to this confrontation with his abandoned daughter. Metis was not part of his plan. He certainly had not intended to free her magics…

That was the part that infuriated her the most. He had bound her magic as a child, limited her, probably for his own fleeting convenience, and hadn't bothered to take the seal off when he left their family home. Had he meant to leave her bound forever? Had he forgotten that he'd even done it?

Let him have a taste of his own medicine.

Metis leaned in closer. "You messed with people I love," she said in a quiet voice.

For the first time, the magister who hated oceans looked afraid.

"Let's start by undoing some of your work," Metis decided. "Take the curses off Captain Bones and Calypso."

"They'll be at the mercy of the island," said Gaulliver, a sly look taking over his face. "My shells protect them now. Are you sure you wish to disrupt that?"

"*Your* shells?" yelled Ianthe, Queen of the Isle of Dream. "The golden seashell is our family crest. You stole my —" she choked on air, putting a hand to the line around her throat.

"Careful, dear," said Gaulliver Seabourne, still smug, damn it, even in ropes. "Don't lose your head."

Metis reached for the nearest teacup. "The island and I have an understanding," she said, tapping her boot against the grass, which rippled a little in response. "It is rather interested in ridding itself of you. You might notice that it has left my crew with their own identities. I suggest you take off the curses you laid upon my friends while I am still prepared to ask nicely."

Gaulliver's eyes glowed briefly gold, and then returned to blue. "Done," he said in a sulky tone.

Metis did not take time to look around and check that Bones and Calypso were all right; she could not afford to be distracted. "And Queen Ianthe," she said steadily.

"Really?" drawled Gaulliver. "You would return the island to her reign of torment and misery?"

"No," Metis said softly. "But I won't deprive Calypso and Orion of a mother."

Gaulliver laughed sharply. "I hate to break it to you, daughter dear, but I'm not the one who laid the curse on the queen. That was my boy."

Metis looked back at Prince Orion. The child stared back at her, wary. "You did this to your mother?" she asked.

The boy shrugged. "Father showed me how."

"A chip off the old block," smirked Gaulliver. "An apprentice any master could be proud of…"

"Please stop talking," Metis sighed. She hadn't meant it to be a spell, but her restored magic was bubbling over, spilling out every which way.

Gaulliver's mouth snapped shut. He looked mortified and enraged.

Interesting. "Don't use your magic for the next twenty four hours," Metis suggested, casting a small embroidered violet which sprouted on the collar of his robes to secure the charmwork in place.

The flying teacups, finally, crashed to the grass.

Calypso ran forward. "Orion, what were you thinking?"

"He said it would be funny," protested the boy. "Do you know how boring it is here? Everyone left. There's only been frogs to talk to for years and years."

"That doesn't mean you can go around cursing our mother's head off!"

Orion stared back, his pale cheeks going pink. "You came back, didn't you? So, it worked."

Calypso looked gutted. "Oh, *kid*."

Queen Ianthe stepped forward, still wearing the gilded seashell crown. "As I have been betrayed by a loved one either way," she snarled. "Can one of you take this curse off me?"

Orion looked terrified. "I'll do it wrong."

"Nonsense," said Metis, coming to her brother's side. "I'll show you how. Unwinding your own spell is much simpler than casting it in the first place, or cracking someone else's."

She whispered for a moment in Orion's ear, giving him the instructions he needed. "Do you understand?"

The boy nodded, and stood straighter. He lifted one hand and pulled, like tugging on a sail rope.

Ianthe screamed, both hands on her throat, and fell to her knees. When she recovered and removed her hands, her throat was unmarked.

Calypso let out a shaky breath. "You're still alive."

"No thanks to you, daughter," snapped the sea witch, getting her feet. "If you and your selfish sisters had not abandoned me, none of this would have happened."

Calypso scoffed. "Oh, really? You were surrounded by daughters when you picked this megalomaniacal magister up off the sand dunes and decided to give him whatever he wanted. You didn't listen to any of us!"

"Mother?" Orion said in a small voice. "What happened to your crown?"

The sea witch flung her grey braids back and lifted one hand to touch her bare head. "The island has decided I am no longer its queen, I suppose," she said with a sniff. "As if I have not been trying to rid myself of that burden for decades."

Gaulliver Seabourne began to laugh, his voice rich and bitter. "My dynasty is assured after all," he said. "Long live the Queen."

Calypso turned around, and an odd expression crossed her face. "Oh, *Bonny*," she said, looking heartbroken.

There was something on Metis' head. She reached up tentatively, telling herself it was just another ornamental galleon, or some other perfectly reasonable…

It was a crown. Of course it was a crown.

Metis snatched it from her head and threw it to the grass. The crown vanished, and she felt it attach itself to her hair, digging into her scalp.

Now the sea witch was laughing, too. "Finally free," Ianthe said, stretching her spine with a satisfying crack.

"Take it back," Metis insisted. "You're fine now, you're not dying, you can——"

Ianthe shook her head slowly. "I was not built for crowns. I have lived for eight decades on this island, serving as its queen. Everyone else got to leave. Why not I?"

"I thought," said Calypso in dismay. "Don't you want us all back here like before? My sisters, our family?"

Her mother gave her a triumphant look. "If I wanted you here, darling girl, I should not have let you go so easily. In a brief moment of magnanimity, I thought it was best to set you all free on the ocean, so you should not be trapped at the mercy of a whimsical magical island with an overactive imagination. Now I am free, I can't find myself caring at all what happens to you. To me, my hunter!"

Ianthe lifted her staff. One of the sea creatures slid out from the mass: part horse, part fish, all blue and silver with glowing eyes. The sea witch took her seat upon its back. "Make your own way out, Calypso, before this island traps you too," she called to her daughter, and surfed away through the trees on a channel of seawater that sprung under the hooves of her steed.

The crown on Metis' head was like a knife to her throat. She stared at Calypso in a panic. "I can't be a queen. I wouldn't know where to start."

"I suppose it's like captaining a ship," Calypso said, equally wide-eyed.

"I can't do that either!" *I don't want to.*

They both looked in desperation to Captain Bones, who reached them in a couple of long strides. "We need to speak to the island," he declared in a warm and reassuring voice. "Full parley."

Metis stared at him. Could he not just scoop her up and take her off in the ship? If ever she needed to be rescued it was right the hell now. "What's a parley?"

"It's a pirate thing," said Calypso, biting her lower lip. "When one ship boards another, or… a captain wants to take someone else's crew-mate. They sit down and negotiate."

"I always thought it would be something you would be rather good at," Bones told Metis. "If we were pirates. You have a knack for talking sense into people."

Metis sighed. "Do you spend a lot of time wondering how we would do things differently if we were pirates instead of privateers?"

Bones gave her a wicked smile that was entirely too charming under the circumstances. "Don't you?"

"It's a good idea," Calypso added. "This island might be one nightmare short of a gothic tragedy. But it respects patterns, rituals. Why else would we hold so many tea parties?"

"Are you saying…" Metis said between her teeth. "… you want to negotiate some kind of trade with the island? For me?"

Bones looked pleased with himself. "I am saying, sweetheart, that this island cannot have you as its queen without me agreeing formally to release you from the *Caliban.* Do you really think that's going to happen?"

(*Sweetheart.*)

"This island swallowed up the entire crew of the *Rosalind* without blinking," Metis said in frustration, not letting him distract her with pet names. "It turned the crew of the *Prosperity* into frogs that are also butlers. What on earth do you think you can say to convince it to release me?"

"You misunderstand," said Bones, reaching out to squeeze your hand. "As your captain, I am well within my rights to call this parley. But I'm not negotiating for your freedom, Metis Seabourne. You are."

15

THERE WAS ONLY ONE SEA CAVE

Calypso led the way. Leaving everyone else at the Summer Palace, she guided Captain Bones and Metis back through the forest, along a rocky outcrop and finally to a small corner of beach where they had not been before.

Water lapped gently into a rivulet leading into a large, imposing sea cave.

"Tell me we won't drown," said Bones in a low voice.

"That's one of the benefits of having a mermaid in your corner," said Calypso, sounding very much like she was trying to keep everyone' spirits up. "Even if this whole cave system filled with water, I would keep you safe."

"That sounds lovely," said Metis. "Let's all look forward to being *nearly* drowned in a cave."

Calypso huffed at her. "This is our best chance to talk to the island. I've never been in here myself — I didn't want to give it ideas. But several of my sisters have. This was siren territory."

There were the remains of nests along the cliff over-hanging this beach — enormous nests. Metis, remembering several ballads describing sirens as fierce bird creatures, did not ask further questions about Calypso's sisters.

"Stop staring at the crown," she muttered to Bones instead. "I can't help it."

Every time she took the thing off, it appeared back on her head. Metis was trying not to think about it. She could not dwell on the possibility that she was going to end up stuck here on this stupid island while Bones and Calypso sailed away on the *Caliban* together.

What would she do? Play endless rounds of croquet with the frog butlers and practice her dance steps in increasingly deranged ballrooms? She might as well have never left home.

(*If Mamma found you turned down a crown, with or without a bridegroom to go with it, she would never forgive you*, said a rather cruel voice very deep inside her.)

The three of them walked over unsteady, slippery rocks and pools, getting deeper and deeper under the island through cave after cave.

"Careful," said Calypso at one point. "It's about to get rather wet."

This next cave was dripping, seawater clinging to its walls and dribbling in slick lines into a wide tide pool covering the cave floor, with only a thin ledge all around. The dominant aesthetic was *sinister*, cheered only by the darting orange flashes of truth fish in the water.

"I thought they might help," said Calypso in a small voice.

"Ah yes, our old friends the truth fish," said Bones dryly. "Blythe… Metis. How do you want to do this?"

Alone, she thought irritably. She hadn't asked either of them to join her. "How do I talk to the island?" she asked

Calypso. The cave caught her words, threw them back in a dull echo.

Island—island—island.

"Thetis would chat away in here for hours," said Calypso. "Doris said she looked into the reflections of the pool until she felt a connection. However you feel most comfortable, I imagine?"

"I'd be comfortable on the deck of the ship," Metis grumbled. She pulled off her boots and striped socks, and stuck her bare feet in the water. Calypso sat to her right, unfurling her tail heavily, and slid forward to splash into the pool up to her waist. The white shirt floated freely in billows on the surface of the water.

Bones took his place on Metis' other side, after pulling off his own boots and socks, so that he could also wet his feet.

If tortured, Metis might admit it was comforting to have them both so near. It might be the last time all three of them were together. Not that there was time for romantic declarations or the breaking of hearts.

"Any good parley starts with voluntary concessions," said Bones.

"I see." Metis thought for a moment, then cleared her throat politely. "Island, would you care to begin by releasing the minds of the crew and passengers of the *Rosalind?* If nothing else, it would be sensible to have Mr Thornbury and the necromancer free to manage our prisoner."

The rock-pool shimmered with a silvery light. Metis saw images in the water: Captain Bell and her sailors returning to their senses. Queen Aud comforting a discombobulated Lady Hadderine. Cousin Mneme, hurling herself into the arms of her spellcracker husband in his flowery coat.

"May I speak with them for a moment?" Metis asked. "As a further gesture of goodwill," she added.

The water sparkled.

"Mneme," Metis spoke, and saw her cousin turn her head to listen. "The magister in ropes may be our kinsman but he kidnapped Queen Aud and has done this island a great wrong. Don't let him escape justice."

She saw Mneme nod and speak hastily to her husband, who whirled around and headed in the direction of the Summer Palace, where Gaulliver Seabourne was still tied up. The pale-eyed necromancer — Bones' brother, wearing an equally silly coat of flowers — followed him.

The images faded.

"Thank you," said Metis to the island. "We can arrange for Mr Seabourne to be taken from this place, and ensure he never sets foot on you again. Is that what you wish?"

The rocks trembled around them. Calypso tipped her head back with a gasp. Her eyes flashed with the same silvery light as the water. "Bring him to the beach," she said in a voice not her own. "We shall take our vengeance, now we know his weakness."

That was Metis' fault, revealing what seawater did to dampen Gaulliver's power. Her father was vulnerable — she had taken his voice and his magic. If the island wanted to hurt him, there was little she could do to stop it. (Did she want to stop it?)

What will the justice of the Teacup Isles even offer? she thought for a moment. *The usual punishment for traitorous magisters is to be imprisoned in the Tower on the Isle of Thyme. Will they give him a cell beside Mamma?*

Bones wrapped his large hand comfortingly around her. Metis remembered him telling her once that his own father had used him as a weapon to hurt others.

"I cannot stop you taking vengeance," she told the island finally. "But I wish you would not." Her feet were in the water with the truth fish, so it couldn't be a lie. Good to know.

Calypso's eyes flashed silver again. "We accept your offer to parley," she said on behalf of the island. "We require a queen. You have been selected."

Metis frowned. Her fingers itched to take the seashell crown off her head again. "You know I don't want it."

Calypso's eyes gleamed brighter. "You do not want it. This mermaid does not want it. The Teacup Queen does not want it. Ianthe has been trying to rid herself of it for centuries. Her salt-struck daughters fled to avoid it. The only one who wants our crown is a man who does not deserve our love." The island sounded rather bitter. Metis did not blame it for that. It hurt, to be unwanted.

Still, she could not make herself *want* to stay here.

A memory flashed through her mind: an awful memory. Miss Metis Seabourne's coming out ball had been awkward and disappointing. Afterwards, when the extended family returned to Storm Bolt for the night, Mamma lectured Metis for over an hour on everything she had done wrong: every way in which she failed to be a perfect lady. So many flaws in how she walked and stood and spoke and danced and didn't dance, and held her tea saucer, and…

Metis fled to another room, on the verge of tears, to find Mneme being browbeaten by Aunt Galatea for her own disappointments: for failing to catch a husband, and refusing to use magic or pretence to do so.

"They mean well," Mneme said later, as the two cousins readied themselves for bed, wrung out with exhaustion.

"Do they?" Metis scowled. "Do they really mean well? Or are

they both miserable because they wish they had two completely different daughters living completely different lives?"

Metis had a good life now. As Bonny Blythe, she had her freedom. She wasn't going to give it up to a tyrannical island with an overactive imagination any more than she was willing to disappear into the life imagined for her by a tyrannical (and as it turned out, somewhat deranged) mamma.

"What do you really want?" she asked the island, feeling desperate. "Surely something better than a reluctant queen moored here against her will. When were you happiest?"

The waters shimmered again, and cleared. A queen rode into view on a bright green horned steed — not Ianthe, a small woman with a magnificent bosom and long blue hair. A crowd rode with this queen, merry folks riding beautiful creatures.

They feasted on a clifftop, eating delicious foods and drinking wines that sparkled with silver and gold. They danced drunkenly in a meadow, slept deeply in a field of poppies, then rose to swim in the sea.

More came: nymphs and fairies, wild inhuman creatures mixing with the Queen and their friends. Laughter. Happiness.

The image shifted to a tea party in the Summer Palace. Its walls glowed with sunshine, sprouting daisies and foxgloves from between every brick. The guests at this party ate sweet cakes and played a mad round of croquet between every round of tiny sandwiches.

Laughter. Happiness.

Metis finally understood.

"You want people to live here and love the worlds you weave for them, to enjoy your — hospitality and food and drink and *magic*. And you've been trying so hard to cling on to the people you have left, you keep driving them away."

The rocks trembled. The images in the pool faded.

"I'm not taunting you," Metis said hastily. "We can fix this. You need to do a better job of using your resources."

"Preferably without stealing my bosun," Captain Bones muttered under his breath.

"Hush, dear," said Metis, absently patting his knee. "They're going to need a bosun. They're going to need a whole crew. Never mind a queen, this island needs a *captain*."

Bones' hand squeezed a little too tightly. "Are you sure…"

"Say on," said not-Calypso, her eyes steady and silver. "Tell us more."

Metis took a deep breath before the ideas spilled out of her. "The Teacup Isles and the Continent are full of people who would love to come here — to live on the island, or to visit. To play games and ride impossible steeds and pick flowers that are the wrong size. The only thing stopping them is having to get past magical storms and enormous portals and jagged rocks to reach you. If the route to the island was more inviting, and you allowed people to come and go as they pleased *without* stealing their memories, you could have an endless supply of merry crowds to keep you company."

"I hear the Isle of Bath is far too crowded over the summer," Bones agreed thoughtfully. "That's why Continental cruises have become so popular."

"Then there are sailors," Metis went on. "Stop building palaces and start building taverns. A coastal town or two with a sturdy dock, and every crew would clamour to spend shore leave on the Isle of Dream."

"It would help if the island gave up its objection to

pirates," considered Bones. "Pirates would eat this place up. Far more spots to bury treasure around here than that pile of bones and rubble we visited recently."

Not-Calypso tilted her head. "You believe what you say."

It was not a question — there were truth fish in the mix.

"When I was a little girl," mused Metis. "I fell in love with a book about a girl called Bonny Blythe who ran away from her family's tea shop to be a pirate captain. She had grand adventures and made new friends, and became famous as the Terror of the Tourmaline Strait. But she missed her family. When she went home, she learned that her family had missed her too. They had moved their teashop to the very edge of the town, overlooking the sea, and turned it into a pirate den, serving gunpowder tea and extremely spicy gingerbread, in the hopes she would come back and visit. And she did. Bonny Blythe came home over and over, at the end of every adventure, because *she was allowed to have everything she wanted*."

Looking back, it was astonishing that her mamma had ever let her read such a subversive tale. Now Metis thought about it, she vaguely remembered it was her papa, who hated the ocean, whose magic was vulnerable to seawater, who bought the first *Adventures of Bonny Blythe* book for her. The same papa who hired a ship of genuine pirates to take him to a magic island…

That was something to think about. Not now. But soon.

"Your words are…" said Calypso-as-the-island, and coughed. Her eyes returned to their usual vivid green. "If we could trust we wouldn't be trapped here, you might even see my sisters again," she said heatedly, addressing the island on her own behalf. "The sea nymphs and the sirens and the witches, and the nereids… we only left because our home had become a prison." She yelped, scrambling out of the water as ice formed on its surface. "Oh, cold!"

Bones and Metis both grabbed Calypso's arms, helping her scramble — legs now, not tail — up on to the rocks between them. They drew their own wet feet up, away from the ice.

"That can't be good," said Metis, eyeing the rock-pool, now thoroughly frozen over. Hopefully the truth fish had been allowed to swim elsewhere before the freeze.

"It's worse," said Bones, nodding towards where there had been a gap between rocks, when they first entered the sea cave. Now it was all rock. "No way out."

"Perhaps they're thinking it over," said Calypso, teeth chattering from the chill.

"Or I offended them so badly that the island is leaving us here to die," said Metis in a panic.

"No, I don't believe it. I *felt* how much the island liked your idea." Calypso was half in Metis' lap, and she turned it into a hug. "You were wonderful. Are you really planning to stay here and manage a series of magical holiday taverns?"

It sounded silly spoken out loud. "I don't know if I'll have a choice," admitted Metis. "At least —" She swallowed. "At least if I have to stay, I can make it a place that the *Caliban* can safely visit."

Calypso rolled her eyes, and exchanged a look with Bones which didn't entirely make sense. "You are *impossible*," she said, and kissed Metis on the mouth.

Metis gasped into it, surprised and yet … she had been waiting to kiss Calypso for a terribly long time. So she kissed back. At least their mouths were warm, even if her fingers still stung from the chill. After a few moments of entirely enjoyable kissing, Calypso pulled away with a happy sigh to glance up, over Metis' shoulder.

"I suppose you want a kiss too," she said with a smile in her voice.

Metis sneaked a glance, wondering what Bones was thinking. It wasn't always easy to tell, but there was a heat in his eyes that felt a lot like Calypso's kiss.

"The truth fish are gone," he said, his voice softer than Metis had ever heard it before. "So I suppose you'll never know…"

Calypso let out a squawk, and pulled him down to her. Now they were both in Metis' lap, her captain and her mermaid, kissing as if they had all the time in the world to get this right.

How can I have ever thought I would let them leave me?

When the lovers turned their attention back to Metis — Bones to lay a trail of searing kisses up the side of her neck, Calypso to tug on the lacings of her striped silk shirt — she was ready for them both.

Time passed. The island might have trapped them in a damp sea cave, but the three of them were able to occupy themselves in an amiable fashion, for some time.

Metis was the first to spot the portal.

She awoke from a light doze to the sound of Bones' heartbeat. She had been using his bare chest for a pillow, and had to take a minute to let that sink in. While she did so, she became very aware of the soft, warm curves of Calypso, pressing along her side.

There was no going back to sleep after that.

She was the only one, therefore, with eyes open wide enough to see when the rock-pool began to emit a gentle glow, golden and familiar.

"I think we have our way out," Metis murmured, kissing Bones on the jaw.

"Let them wait," he muttered, and found her mouth with his own.

Some time after that, the three of them — dressed properly again, with boots, belts and breeches in some semblance of order — stood on the edge of the rock-pool, gazing down into the golden portal.

"Whatever happens," said Calypso. "Whatever is waiting for us on the other side of this. We can handle it. We're the best crew in the Lyric Sea."

"I think," said Bones in a low growl. "If the two of you can stop trying to sacrifice yourselves long enough for us to get our ship back, we can't lose."

Metis said nothing. She had said everything she wanted to, for now.

Hand in hand, the three of them stepped into the portal, bracing themselves for whatever the Isle of Dream had to throw at them next.

16

———

IF WE SHADOWS HAVE
OFFENDED

WINE WITH MRS SEABOURNE

"*O*h," said Calypso, with a breathy laugh that made Metis want to kiss her all over again. "This is much better than palaces."

The Isle of Dream had been busy.

While Metis and her lovers lingered in the sea cave, the island had taken on quite a rapid transformation. Just past the sand dunes where Metis had rescued Ginger from the hen party, a brand new pier had appeared with fresh-painted planks, leading out to a friendlier bay than before. Not nearly as many jagged rocks!

There were taverns, wide and welcoming, bearing names such as Pirate's Rest, Siren Song, and New Prosperity, right on the beach, overlooking the pier.

There was a tea shop with a skull and bones pattern on the curtains, and a gift shop featuring cheerful souvenirs from the Isle of Dream. The island was ready to welcome tourists to its shores.

There were docks, sturdy and secure, ready to fill with ships (and there was one very familiar ship there already, upright and ready to sail).

When Bones spotted the *Caliban*, he let out a shuddering breath like someone had gut-punched him,

Calypso gave him an encouraging shove. "Go and look her over. We'll get the drinks in."

Bones gave them both a winning smile and headed off for his ship.

Metis wanted to run after him, but there were still matters to settle on the island. She pushed open the swinging doors of the New Prosperity.

It looked like any other tavern she had visited since becoming a privateer — perhaps a little grander than most, with palatial high windows like those from the Ruined Palace, and the nameplate of the original ship *Prosperity* buried in the flagstones of the wall.

"Metis!" cried a familiar voice, and her cousin Mneme ran at her for an embrace. "Are you well, have you been well?" she asked, looking her over. "I've been so worried. I've missed you."

"I missed you too," Metis said with a laugh. It was true enough, even without tiny peach fish to force the admission from her. "I've been busy, and well. So well. This is Calypso, my—" Her bravery abandoned her for a moment.

Calypso didn't hesitate. "Girlfriend," she said firmly, greeting Mneme with a sailor's handshake. "Lovely to meet you, Mrs Seabourne. May I buy you a drink?"

Things blurred after that. There was chatter and smiles — Doc Smedley was there, and Ginger, both coming over to check that Metis and Calypso were all right — there was a long conversation about wine and whether or not a magical island could conjure up specific vintages, or if it had to let them age honestly.

Metis could not entirely believe that her two worlds had collided and nothing had shattered; nothing awful had been said. Mneme was quite charmed by Calypso, and there was no shortage of topics for the two to chat about — Metis didn't even mind too much when she overhead her cousin telling embarrassing childhood anecdotes to her beautiful, confident mermaid girlfriend.

Some while later, when Captain Bones strode into the tavern with Hobsbawn and Sal, talking enthusiastically about how the Isle of Dream had appeared on their charts, he paused briefly to catch Metis into his arms and kiss her breathless before heading to the bar, where he did the same to Calypso.

Metis snuck a look over at Mneme, preparing herself to see an expression of shock or disapproval on her face. She knew her cousin wasn't Mamma or Aunt Galatea, but still…

Mrs Mnemosyne Seabourne sipped her wine thoughtfully, and raised her glass in a silent toast to her cousin, across the tavern.

So that was all right, then.

~

RETIREMENT FOR LADIES

Captain Elizah Bell of the *Rosalind* surveyed the taproom of the New Prosperity with great satisfaction. "I always planned to run a tavern when I retired," she said.

"You want to stay?" said Metis in astonishment.

"Why wouldn't I? Most fun I've had in years. And that

last sea storm…" Bell whistled under her breath. "Not going to top that in another decade of sailing."

"What about your ship? Your crew?"

Bell shrugged. "Magic or no magic, my old ship's been taken apart too many times for us to trust she's seaworthy. Queen Aud has agreed to retire the *Rosalind* from service. Her Majesty will sail home on the *Caliban*, and Captain Bones can take any of my crew who need a ride home. There's a few of us planning to stay — my ship's surgeon wants to study the coastal flora for a book she's writing, and some of my older seadogs are eyeing off the opportunities of a new settlement like this."

"I will also be staying," interrupted Lady Hadderine Bustledown in a prim voice. "I have informed her Majesty that it's time for her to select a new Mistress of the Robes."

Mneme looked astonished. "Really, my lady?"

"Indeed," said the elderly lady-in-waiting. "My grandmamma — who served in the royal household herself until she was eighty one years old — always said that retirement was the greatest adventure of all, but I never believed her until now. All that awaited me at Wistworia Palace was the prospect of curating an exhibit of my old bonnets for the palace museum. Whereas here, I may manage a delightful little gift shop and spend my free time perfecting my croquet game."

Bell pulled a pint of cider into a crystal tankard, topped it off with several brandied cherries and a slice of pineapple on a stick, and handed it to Lady Hadderine, who downed it in three magnificent gulps.

"Oh, yes," said Lady Hadderine. "That hits the spot."

Metis had a troubling thought that there might be some of the *Caliban* crew who likewise wanted to jump ship to take advantage of this rapidly growing oceanic resort, and then she had another thought, like a bolt of lightning.

"Captain Bell," she said, hardly daring to hope. "Do you think, perhaps… if you are absolutely set on staying here…"

I can't be a queen. I wouldn't know where to start.

I suppose it's like captaining a ship.

The grey-haired captain gave her a wicked grin, showing off several gold-capped teeth, and flexed her biceps a little. "Go on, then," she said. "Give it a go."

Carefully, Metis lifted the seashell crown from her head and placed it on the head of the captain of the *Rosalind* (retired).

"How do I look?" asked Captain Bell.

Mneme applauded politely.

Lady Hadderine reached out, and adjusted the crown to sit at a more rakish angle. "Exquisite, my dear," she said with approval. "Just right."

Captain Bell winked at her.

Mneme nudged Metis with a remarkably sharp elbow. "I'd go and find that captain and mermaid of yours, if I were you," she remarked. "Let them know you don't have to be queen any more."

Metis nodded wildly. "I will," she said. "I will." She couldn't quite bring herself to move off her stool. "In a minute. When I believe it myself."

A NECROMANCER AND A PRIVATEER WALK INTO A BAR

"Dom," said Captain Bones, greeting his brother in the doorway of the New Prosperity.

"Will," said the necromancer with the creepy pale eyes. He was a few inches shorter than Bones, with lighter hair and no sign of a beard. He had managed to rid himself of the costume of a flower knight, and was now garbed in pirate blacks in leather and silk not a million miles from what his brother wore.

He looked like a dangerous man, but that wasn't news to Metis.

(She suspected the necromancer's costume change had something to do with the Treasure Chest, the latest shop that had appeared in the spreading township. The island had always liked dressing people up. Ginger was still combing the shop's racks, searching for any sign of the red dress she had worn while briefly brainwashed into being a lounge singer. "No frock left behind!" she howled when Sal tried to convince her it was time to give up.)

Metis observed the brothers from a respectful distance, knowing that they needed to discuss the logistics of how the dangerous prisoner Gaulliver Seabourne was to be transported safely back to the Teacup Isles. They didn't need the daughter of said prisoner putting her oar in.

Currently, the brothers were busily *not* saying an awful lot to each other, and that sort of conversation was best done without interruptions too.

Still, when Bones glanced in her direction and said "Metis, what do you think?" she couldn't help but feel warm all over.

"I think it would be best if you kept my father as far away from me and my magic as possible," she said honestly, and was rewarded by an approving look from the necromancer before the two brothers headed out to make the arrangements.

~

QUEEN AUD AND HER MANTICORE

The Isle of Dream, so enthusiastic when it came to spontaneously generating infrastructure for its future as the Top Holiday Spot of the Lyric Sea (as recommended by 4 out of 5 swashbuckling scallywags), had largely stopped responding to personal requests.

The island had restored the minds and identities and true shapes of nearly every current inhabitant of the island, including most of the frog butlers (formerly the crew of the *Prosperity*). After being restored to their human selves, three had requested a return to their frog butler shapes as a matter of preference.

In the meadow behind the new town, Mr Thornbury Seabourne, celebrated spellcracker, was put to work tidying up the last of the loose ends, which included restoring a giant glass hedgehog to its natural size.

Next, Thornbury set about transforming the multi-coloured manticore from the Queen's hunt back into the human form of Alfred, Lord Manticore.

This took longer than anyone expected. After several failed attempts, Thornbury was down to undershirt and long-johns, sweating in the sunshine (he had not yet been granted the leisure to replace his floral knight attire with something more sensible at the Treasure Chest) and utterly drained.

Queen Aud waited nearby, wringing her hands with worry. In the absence of her recently retired Mistress of the Robes, Calypso had offered the young queen a shoulder to cry on.

As Thornbury took a moment to rest, Mneme brought over a flask of lemonade to slake his thirst. "You don't look well," she said, concerned for her husband. "Perhaps you should wait a few hours before trying again."

Metis coughed discreetly. "Can I help?"

Thornbury wiped his brow with his discarded tabard, the one covered in embroidered buttercups. "Do you think you could speak to the island again?"

"No, I mean…" Awkwardly, she approached him and stuck out her hand. Surprised, Thornbury clasped it at the elbow, magister-style, as if they were old school chums. His eyes widened. "Miss Seabourne, did you always have this amount of magic?"

Metis understood his surprise. They had first met at her cousin's house party, where Thornbury's job was preventing young ladies from using magic on the Duke of Storm. He had barely given Metis a second glance back then, not registering her as much of a threat to his employer.

"It's a long story," she said. "But take what you need. It's all in the family."

Nodding, he replenished his magic with hers, and went back to work.

It was past supper time when Lord Manticore was finally restored to his tall and grumpy human form. They had drawn quite a crowd by then, folks bringing out food, drinks and lanterns so as to observe the proceedings. Metis was seated on a fallen log with Captain Bones while they shared a surprisingly good bowl of oyster stew from one of the newly grown taverns.

Lord Manticore's suit was damp, and his black hair had gone quite fluffy in the process. He looked exhausted and put upon and annoyed, but no more than usual.

"Alfred!" burst out Queen Aud, and ran at him like a cat after a dragonfly, hurling herself into his arms in reckless abandon. He caught her with a bemused looking expression, submitting to the embrace despite their audience.

"Will you stop now," she murmured, peppering his face with small kisses. "Telling me to marry other people?"

Lord Manticore winced. "It's for the good of the kingdom," he muttered.

Queen Aud poked him in the ribs. "Perhaps you could also stop telling me what's good for the kingdom. This wouldn't have happened if we were safely married."

Metis opened her mouth to argue, given that her wretched father paid little heed to formal marriage agreements and probably would have arranged Queen Aud's kidnapping even if she had six husbands at home. Calypso, wandering over to join Metis and Bones on the log, gave her a mocking look as if she knew what she was thinking.

It was probably best to let the Queen have her moment without additional commentary.

"I won't do it," said Queen Aud, kneeling before the man she loved. "No more secret conferences with princes, no more contracts and treaties and 'for the good of the kingdom'. I will not sacrifice the possibility of happiness. I will marry no one but you, even if it means the Teacup Isles fall into war!"

Bones leaned in to Metis from her other side. "That's exciting," he murmured in a deadpan tone. "War means plenty of work for privateers."

Calypso gave them both a wicked grin. "We're allowed to act like pirates in a time of war. Boarding ships and taking booty…"

"Settle down, both of you," Metis said sternly. "I'm sure it was romantic hyperbole."

Clearly it was romantic *something*, as Lord Manticore was now kissing the Queen without hesitation, and she had her arms wound around his neck in triumph.

~

A PROPER INTRODUCTION

They began loading the *Caliban* at dawn. Metis was glad to be back where she belonged, though figuring out where to put all their extra crew and passengers was a logistical nightmare.

The quartermaster of the *Rosalind* started a whisper campaign to oust Ginger from her position, and found himself mysteriously tied to the mast by a pair of stockings.

Queen Aud, blissfully betrothed, did not hesitate to take the captain's cabin for herself, which scuppered quite a few romantic plans Metis and Calypso had brewing for the voyage home.

Now that normality was somewhat restored, Queen Aud started hinting that Calypso would make an excellent Mistress of the Robes, should she wish to move permanently to Wistworia Palace. This brought out a remarkable streak of possessiveness in Metis and led to some melodramatic kissing in the galley before Rafferty kicked them out.

Mneme soothed the waters in her usual calming manner, Ginger volunteered the cabin sprats to help out with hair and laundry, and the crisis passed.

Mneme escaped the Queen long enough to corner Metis. "You still haven't introduced me to your young man," she said with a stern look.

"You've met him," said Metis in surprise. "I saw you talking to him earlier, after he stopped you being knocked overboard by those barrels. You really shouldn't be on deck, you know, before we are ready to sail…"

Her cousin gave her an extremely aunt-like expression. "Metis Seabourne!"

"Yes, all right," Metis grumbled, and snagged Bones' coat sleeve next time he went past. It was rather gratifying, the way that he stopped what he was doing if she even hinted that she needed his attention.

"What's up, love?" he asked, eyes full of good humour.

Metis dusted off her garden party manners. "Mrs Mnemosyne Seabourne, may I introduce my captain, J. Willoughby Bones?"

"Charmed," said Bones, kissing Mneme's hand in a manner that was almost but not entirely rogueish. "I've done some work with your husband over the years."

"I'm sure you have," said Mneme in a knowing voice. (Metis was going to have to grill them both later, to find out what exactly they weren't saying about the nature of Thornbury's work.)

"I believe you're related to my sister-in-law, the Duchess of Storm?" Bones went on, like they were greeting each other at a ball and not at all like he had recently seized hold of Mneme's waist to move her out of the way when three barrels of fresh water had been rolled along the deck at unexpected speed.

"She married our cousin Henry," said Mneme, still dripping with politeness. "Captain Bones, may I ask you a favour?"

He grinned his warmest and most charming grin. It made Metis want to rip his shirt off. "As long as you don't plan to lure my bosun back home with you, Mrs Seabourne, you may have unlimited favours."

"Please introduce me to your brother," said Mneme. "Fully and formally."

A few minutes later, a terrifying necromancer was added to the Really Truly Not a Garden Party, Oops, Please Duck So You Don't Get Decapitated By That Sail.

"There you are, Dom!" said Bones. "May I introduce Mrs Mnemosyne Seabourne, cousin to my… bosun. Mrs

Seabourne, this is my brother Mr Dominic Von Trask, Twelfth Magister Circle, First Crescent.”

The necromancer gave them both a bemused look, then looked to Metis as if she might provide some explanation of this nonsense. She shrugged, having no more idea than he did. “We’ve met, Mrs Seabourne,” he said finally. “We came here on the *Rosalind* together.”

“We have not *formally* met, Mr Von Trask,” said Mneme, pronouncing his last name with relish.

The necromancer gave a surprisingly pleasant smile. “Oh, please. We’re practically related. Do call me Dominic.”

AN AWFULLY BIG ADVENTURE

There was, of course, the problem of what to do with Prince Orion, given that his father was about to be tried for treason and magical malfeasance, and his mother had sea witched herself who-knew-where.

Calypso and Metis cornered him in the tea shop, where the boy had managed to acquire a sticky bun almost the size of his head.

After an awkward introduction of Metis as his other sister, Calypso broached the question: “We were wondering if you want to come with us, on the *Caliban*.”

The boy stared suspiciously at them both, chewing. “Can I be a pirate?”

He had clearly visited the Treasure Chest recently with this goal in mind. He was dressed as the world’s smallest pirate, all bright red kerchief, skull-printed shirt, and slashed pantaloons.

"We're not pirates, we're privateers," said Metis. "We work for the Crown."

Orion scowled. "But if I come with you, we *might* get raided by pirates?"

"Probably not," said Metis, at the same time that Calypso said:

"Pretty regularly."

"Wait," said Metis. "Really?"

"Have you not been boarded by pirates yet?" Calypso looked surprised. "It's been over a year, Bonny, what have you been doing with yourself?"

"I've not been boarded by pirates, that's what I've been doing."

Orion finished his bun while they bickered. "Can I be first mate?"

"No," Metis and Calypso said in unison.

"You'd start as a cabin sprat," said Metis. "Until you get promoted to able seaman. Or kidnapped by pirates, whichever comes first. We could send you to boarding school," she added thoughtfully, remembering that Seabournes did have other options for taking care of neglected children. "But your chances of being kidnapped by pirates would be greatly reduced."

Orion shrugged. "All right. Cabin sprat. Could be worse."

~

GETTING MATEY

"No, cap'n," said Sal in frustration. "You can't have two first mates!"

The *Caliban* had been at sea for three hours. The waters were remarkably calm, considering what the journey inward had been like.

Calypso and Sal had just realised how Captain Bones was planning to resolve the staffing situation, and neither of them were happy about it.

"You can't give me my old job back," Calypso complained. "I left. And your crew works perfectly well without me. I don't mind going back to the ranks."

"I can step aside," said Sal. "It's fine!"

"Sal could be bosun again," suggested Metis, willing to make the sacrifice.

"No!" chorused Calypso, Sal and Bones.

"If everyone could just take a short holiday from throwing themselves on swords," thundered Bones. "This is a ridiculous ship and I am an imperfect captain and some-times I need two people to tell me how wrong I am! You're it." He pointed at Sal, and Calypso.

Metis coughed and looked at the sky.

"Three people," her captain said, calming down some-what. "Three people to tell me how wrong I am. Except right now. I will accept no discussion about this particular command decision."

"Ginger," Sal called out. "This is your territory. You speak for the crew."

Ginger, who was lying in a deckchair under an enor-mous umbrella with a cocktail, waved cheerfully. "The crew took a vote," she informed them. "They reckon it's fine to have two first mates."

~

CROW'S NEST

The crow's nest was not designed for three people to sit in comfortably, even three people who rather enjoyed being squashed together in an improbable space.

They managed it, though. For the two weeks it took to sail from the Isle of Dream all the way to the Isle of Town, this was the closest that Metis and Bones and Calypso would get to any privacy.

(Metis had hastily taught herself several new safety charms to ensure that nothing untoward would happen to her captain or her mermaid.)

It had been mooted that the *Caliban* could drop off her passengers at the Isle of Nemesis, which they reached after only six days at sea. The passengers could then have used portals to return the Queen to the capital more efficiently. But Queen Aud, cozily ensconced in the captain's cabin with Lord Manticore, insisted this was the closest thing she was likely to get to a honeymoon, and she was in no hurry to return to the palace.

(As ship's captain, Bones had married the Queen to her Minister three days into the voyage. Rafferty was outraged that no one had given him sufficient notice to make a wedding cake, and was still passive aggressively sugaring almonds in the galley.)

They were now twenty-four hours out from the Isle of Town. Almost there. Soon they would have their ship back (and their private cabin) and the new normal for the *Caliban* could properly begin.

Still, there was something to be said for this — three people squashed into a crow's nest, drinking a fresh pot of Siren Song from tin mugs (the porcelain cups had been seconded by the queen) and enjoying each other's company for a few quiet moments before the next bell.

Calypso hummed a shanty under her breath, twisting Metis' blue hair into tiny braids. Metis tipped her head back, gazing at the stars. They were so bright out here. Brighter than you ever saw them from land.

Bones traced a pattern on her wrist with his fingertip. It was the spot that Metis had picked for her first tattoo. She had been teasing them both for days by not telling them what design she had been working on with the ship's surgeon.

"Bosun Blythe," he murmured.

"Mmm?" She tilted her head to meet his dark, dancing eyes. "Captain Bones?"

"Do you fancy running away to sea with us?"

She smiled. "That seems dangerous. Will there be sharks?"

"Sometimes."

"Mermaids?"

(Calypso kissed Metis on the neck and giggled.)

"If you're very lucky," said Bones.

Metis let out a heavy sigh. "I'm not sure if I can. I have appointments with the dressmaker, and the dance instructor, and I'm due to attend sixteen balls next week."

"That is a lot of balls," Bones said gravely. "Are you sure I can't tempt you? We can offer adventure, excitement, a high risk of scurvy and a whole lot of deck swabbing."

Metis pretended to consider. "I do enjoy deck swabbing."

"Also foot rubs," volunteered Calypso. "And kisses."

There was a brief pause in the conversation, for demonstrative purposes.

"I'm not sure it's proper," Metis said, when she had her breath back, "for a young lady to run away to sea. Whatever might happen to me?"

"Everything," growled Captain Bones. "If we're lucky."

17

CORRESPONDENCE FROM THE CALIBAN

FROM: BOSUN BLYTHE ON HER MAJESTY'S PRIVATEER *CALIBAN*

TO: MRS MNEMOSYNE SEABOURNE, TEMPEST MANSE, NORTH VILLAGE, ISLE OF STORM

Dear Mneme,

See, I can write lttrs! Ink is low, will be brf. Thank you for the news of Henry and Jun. I prom. I'm not avoiding them, & will visit when their invits are for anything other than balls or grden parties.

I sent a gift for the baby: haven't lost all my manners.

Thank you also for the gift of Seabourne Bramble — hadn't realised how much I missed 'proper' tea from home, & have been drinking it all week instead of U. Tears, Rafferty has been giving me some very strange looks & when I tried to give him a taste he refused on the grnds he doesn't believe apples exist. Just what you want to hear from a ship's cook.

I'm writing now because the Qn is sending the *Caliban* on a mission to Cape Sycorax to fetch some [secret matter] from a [covert location] so if you don't hear from me for a few mnths, don't worry.

We're due for extnded shore leave after that, & likely to be spending next summ. on the I. of Dream if you & Thornbury fancy a jaunt to the seaside. I know you literally already live at the seaside but does your seaside feature twelve magical tverns & what is reported to be the best chip shop south of the Troil. Empire? I don't think so!

(We've heard rumrs that sirens have returned to the isle & Calypso is hoping to be reunited with some stray family members, so it might be fun to have some of my stray family members along for the ride. I suppose He. & Ju. and little C. won't quite be ready for a Grand Tour, but they're more than welcome. D. Von Tr was non-committal, which almost crtainly means he's coming.)

I have to run. Ori. has been swbbing the deck for the last 2 hours & doing it all wrong & Bones says I need to be less sarcastic around the kid while he's learning new skills, so I'm going to go hide in the galley & be sarcastic at Raff. instead. He can take it!

Hope you're enjoying your new house with all its curtains & sideboards & whatnot. Sounds lovely. <u>Not sarcasm</u>! We will visit one of these days (Ori. is demanding visitation rights to Bas. the hdghg) but you might want to give the btler & suchlike a day off as anyone I drag into your house is bound to be terribly shocking to their snsibilities.

My cptain & mermd send their love to you & your spllcracker. Or. says don't forget to feed Bas. more kelp.

Your salty & seaworthy coz,
Metis Seabourne, Bonny Blythe
xxx

THE END.

ABOUT THE AUTHOR

Tansy Rayner Roberts is an award-winning Australian fantasy author. She has been a co-host of the epic all-female Doctor Who podcast *Verity!* for more than a decade. Tansy blames Arthur Ransome for her childhood obsession with fictional boats and *Black Sails* for her adult obsession with pirates. She lives with her family in Tasmania.

- Listen to Tansy on Sheep Might Fly, a podcast where she reads aloud her stories as audio serials.
- Read Tansy's stories before anyone else when you pledge to her Patreon.
- What tea is Tansy drinking? Find out when you subscribe to her excellent newsletter: tinyurl. com/tansyrr
- Follow Tansy on Bookbub so you never miss a release.

facebook.com/TansyRRoberts

instagram.com/tansyrr

patreon.com/tansyrr

bookbub.com/authors/tansy-rayner-roberts

ALSO BY TANSY RAYNER ROBERTS

TEACUP MAGIC

Tea & Sympathetic Magic

The Frost Fair Affair

Spellcracker's Honeymoon

Lady Liesl's Seaside Surprise

Have Spirit, Will Duchess

This Enchanted Island

SPARKS & PHILTRES

Gate Sinister

House Perilous

Land Glorious

THE RIVER DIVINE

Of Knives & Night-blooms

THE CREATURE COURT

Power & Majesty

The Shattered City

Reign of Beasts

Cabaret of Monsters

BELLADONNA U

Unreal Alchemy

Holiday Brew

Practical Witching

MUSKETEER SPACE

Musketeer Space

Joyeux

Time of the Cat

Castle Charming

Castle Ever After

Gorgons Deserve Nice Things

Siren Beat

Love & Romanpunk

Splashdance Silver

Liquid Gold

Ink Black Magic

<u>NON-FICTION & ESSAYS</u>

Pratchett's Women: Unauthorised Essays

From Baby Brain to Writer Brain: Writing Through A World Of Parenting Distractions

It's Raining Musketeers

<u>AS EDITOR</u>

Mother of Invention (with Rivqa Rafael)

Cranky Ladies of History (with Tehani Croft)

Adventures Across Space and Time: A Doctor Who Reader
(with Paul Booth, Matt Hills & Joy Piedmont)

www.ingramcontent.com/pod-product-compliance
Lightning Source LLC
Chambersburg PA
CBHW010642190726
48289CB00009B/2822